PRA

"A deftly-told story of a young woman with amnesia investigating her own past. It's beguiling, haunting, beautifully paced and it kept me hooked to the very end." MICHAEL WALTERS, AUTHOR OF *THE COMPLEX*

"Annalisa Crawford's story is intense in emotion and does a good job of taking suspense in an intellectual direction. It links a strong mystery plot with a mesmerizing level of detail in Jo's mind because the mystery she has to solve is about herself. While it's a big challenge for Jo to be a detective when the clues are all embedded in her literally mind-numbing lack of memory, it's a delight for a reader to be swept along in the process with her. It's both poignant and action-packed. I couldn't put this book down because the creepy, fascinating concept of someone slowly having their memories resurface was so compelling and well shown. A talented work of fiction, *Small Forgotten Moments* builds minute-by-minute tension to a gripping conclusion as Jo's confused, yet assertive personality swirls from the pages much like the vividly described art of Zenna that she creates." SARAH SCHEEL, *READERS' FAVORITE*

"A soulful tale of painting, secrets, and longing, which draws the reader into a world of mystery and memory. Filled with the colors of an artist's mind and set against the wild backdrop of the Cornwall coast—an enchanting read." LEONORA MERIEL, AUTHOR OF *THE UNITY GAME*

"A spellbinding, intoxicating journey into the dark heart of obsession. Annalisa Crawford has penned another beautiful, heart-wrenching, epic masterpiece. I loved it." TOM GILLESPIE, AUTHOR OF *THE STRANGE BOOK OF JACOB BOYCE*

About the Author

Annalisa Crawford lives in Cornwall, UK, with a good supply of moorland and beaches to keep her inspired. She lives with her husband, two sons, and canine writing partner, Artoo. She is the author of four short story collections and two novels.

www.annalisacrawford.com

SMALL
FORGOTTEN
MOMENTS

ANNALISA
CRAWFORD

www.vineleavespress.com

Small Forgotten Moments
Copyright © 2021 Annalisa Crawford
All rights reserved.

Print Edition
ISBN: 978-1-925965-65-0
Published by Vine Leaves Press 2021

Cover design by Jessica Bell
Interior design by Amie McCracken

 A catalogue record for this book is available from the National Library of Australia

For my sister, Kimberley

ONE

David Bowie sings "Suffragette City" from the corner of the room and my bare, paint-splattered feet stomp out the beat. I square up to the easel with my brush loaded with Winsor Blue.

My hand hovers in mid-air.

A blank canvas is full of possibility, a foe to be vanquished. The first mark will determine the shape of the whole thing—the style and tone and subject. Why am I finding it so hard?

When I woke this morning, far too early, I was flooded with images and my hands itched for my paints. I skipped breakfast. My first mug of coffee is cold on the table.

But those ideas have dissipated. I trail the brush down the canvas, creating tentative vertical lines. Some are solid and uniform, others dawdle erratically, tapering toward the bottom to create the illusion of rain. With my new tube of Crimson, I draw a dense crowd—vague anthropoid outlines squeezed together, the suggestion of faces, all looking toward the top right-hand corner. I avoid anything specific, anything that could be *her*. Where the colors intersect, deep violet occurs.

I spurt Azo Yellow Medium onto my palette and add spots and streaks to resemble streetlights and reflections in puddles.

Wham bam, thank you Ma'am.

It's a fussy and congested mess now—the doodle of a child let loose with poster paints for the first time. I run an acrylic-sticky hand through my hair, tugging at the purple knot which forms.

Shards of light stream through the window as the sun sneaks out from looming rain clouds, catching the wet paint and animating the figures.

Here she comes, here she comes.

From the canvas, *she* stares back, sculpted and detached like a *Vanity Fair* cover model.

Her. Zenna. She smirks because she's not supposed to be here. I splash color onto the canvas, eradicating her with my paint-loaded brush. She raises her hand and blows a kiss.

"Stop it! Leave me alone!"

I throw the painting to the floor. It hits the corner of my coffee table—dented, ruined. I screw my hands into a fist, holding back from sweeping all the tubes and brushes onto the floor.

Nathan stands at the door, jacket on, bag slung over his shoulder.

I unfurl my fingers from the fist and take long breaths, counting back from ten until—theoretically—when I reach one, I'm calm and poised. Nathan taught me that; he said my artistic temperament would get me into trouble.

"It's going well, then?"

I scowl at the naked easel and mutter to myself.

"Are you still working on exhibition pieces? Surely it's too late now?"

"I was trying to start something new, something *different.*"

"Oh." And that *oh* makes my heart sink because it means he sees Zenna as clearly as I do.

The picture lies dying at my feet. The colors on my palette are raucous and grating. The music is suddenly clamorous and engulfing. I lean to switch it off as Major Tom floats away and there's a vacuum—the silence whispers to me.

"Are you up early, or very late?"

I glance at the clock: half past eight. My stomach grumbles for breakfast. "Up early. Have you just got home?"

"Yeah."

"So, it's going well, you and—?"

"Simone." He shrugs and heads to the kitchen. "It's only been a couple of dates. I don't know yet. Coffee? Are you working today?"

"Yes, please. No, day off." I follow him, gouging my heel into Zenna's cheek on my way past. I feel victorious for a second or so.

"You look awful. You should probably get some rest before this evening."

"Well, thanks—just what I wanted to hear."

I open the cupboard and flick through the boxes of cereal. Hungry but not wanting food. I take a slice of ham from the fridge and tear it into bite-sized pieces.

"It'll be okay, you know."

"What will?" Zenna's lurking, distracting me—creeping in the shadows. I glance behind me, almost expecting her to be waiting in the doorway.

"The exhibition. Your painting. You'll get tonight out of the way and move on to the next project." He hands me a mug. "Have you got any idea what that will be?"

"Abstract. Something very abstract."

With a half-wave of surrender, I shuffle to my room. I lack the energy to remain upright, to concentrate on conversation; my eyes refuse to focus. In bed, I hear the downstairs people moving around, and the Radio 4 News carrying up through the floor, and the indistinct hum of planes soaring into the sky, and the hurried footsteps of straggling school kids. The noise diminishes as I eventually drift to sleep.

***

Painting Zenna over and over wasn't intentional. In the beginning, I had no concept of what I was creating, I just allowed the paints to flow, the ideas to flower. An almost ethereal creature materialized before me. Like a sprite or fairy. So different from my usual style. I relished every session, couldn't wait to get home from work and throw on my painting shirt. It was exhilarating.

Usually a portrait is planned. The subject has commissioned you because they're aware of your work and like it, or you've sought out fascinating faces and pleaded with them to sit for you. You'll have taken photos to work from or have them posing in front of you. Not so with the woman who appeared beneath my brush—I had no clue who she was.

Once I started, I couldn't stop. Every new piece was a variation of Zenna, telling a story of sadness and longing, of melancholy and hopelessness. I was compelled, driven to recreate this immersive creature time and again. As one painting was propped against the wall to dry, another began.

In one fugue state, I drew her in charcoal. Broken shards were strewn across the floor, as though I'd been frenzied and hurried; black dust coated the paper and stained my fingers. She stared deep into my eyes—too real, too beguiling. Burrowing into my head, skulking into my mind, breaching the barrier into my soul. I threw the sketchpad aside and buried it beneath my pillows. The room had grown icy; I was shivering. I needed a hot shower, but my hands reached for another page.

"You should take a break," Nathan said more than once. "Come and eat. You look like you haven't slept in days."

I stared at him, his face merging with Zenna's until I was uncertain who was talking to me. I probably hadn't slept. His words were slurred and deep like a record being played far too slow. Despite his insistence, I continued.

One of the early pictures—*Blue Woman*—was bought almost immediately. Nathan had posted a photo of me at my easel on Instagram for one of his 'check out my weird roommate' updates, and my benefactor contacted him.

In the picture, I'm intent on my work, oblivious to Nathan hovering around me. My hair is a curly mop streaked with French Ultramarine where I'd repeatedly tucked a brush behind my ear. I'm molding my face into different expressions in front of a mirror because I was attempting a self-portrait. How long ago it all seems.

The shape of my face was wrong, and I couldn't rectify it. The complexion was too pale, the countenance almost regal; the whole essence of myself was missing. I persisted, curious to see what—who—would emerge. I painted until my eyes were blurry and my arms too exhausted to hold the brush, and Nathan had to guide me to bed.

Blue Woman was the result.

She was familiar—a face from my dreams or my unremembered past. I have no sense of when she became Zenna, or of ever naming her. I just knew it was who she was.

I return to the photo occasionally—copied and saved onto my laptop from Nathan's Instagram. It's the beginning, after all, the origin. The offer of an exhibition in a tiny gallery in the city came from it—my first show—so I'm grateful. Zenna, it appears, is my lucky charm.

***

This gallery, this exhibition. Tonight.

With its sharp white walls and high ceiling, all I want to do is scream. I need to hear my voice echo, want it to spin around the room and carry me to Kansas. The more I think about shouting, the closer I am to doing so. I chew my lip to suppress random exclamations from bursting out. I grab Nathan's arm, to keep myself grounded.

I've already spent several days here, overseeing the placement of the paintings, checking the view from different angles, scrutinizing the way they were removed from their crates and examining them for any damage. I've walked around this room and trailed my hand across the canvases, tracing the crevices and ridges of the acrylic, absorbing the almost magical atmosphere of the empty room.

They're smaller and less striking than when I was working on them—adrift, flanked by the stark expanse of wall. I've been to galleries where I've gazed up and up, and the piece has enveloped me. My work almost shies away; the opposite of when they were on my easel at home.

Slowly, I revolve on my stiletto heels. I hadn't appreciated the discomfort of so many eyes following me around the room. No matter where I am or how quickly I move, she's right there. Nathan is unaffected; the staff and caterers are busy with the final touches. I rub warmth into my arms and wish I'd worn a jacket.

Nathan hands me a glass of wine from the long cloth-covered table near the entrance.

"Are we allowed this now?"

"You're the artist; you're allowed anything you want."

I sip quickly. We're early. It was my suggestion—I thought I'd be less anxious without the panic of rushing through the city traffic. As I'm currently in a flouncy evening dress and heels I can barely walk in, I realize being late was only a small part of my angst.

Nathan flicks my glass with his fingernail. It tings. "Slow down."

"I'm nervous, if you hadn't noticed. This is a bad idea. Who am I, anyway? Just a nobody artist who should be sitting at home in her pajamas." I bounce on my toes and finish my drink in three mouthfuls.

Guests trickle in, to spend their Tuesday evening in a small art gallery on a back road just off Piccadilly. They take catalogues and glasses of wine from the table at the entrance and pretend to be interested. I'm nudged around, in the way, side-stepping everyone until I locate a quiet corner. Hiding is good—if only I could remain here all evening.

Opposite me, *Zenna in the Sea*, the unanticipated centerpiece, is lit with soft spotlights so when people walk in, they're drawn in her direction.

At first, she wasn't in the sea at all. Without it, she was a woman gazing with glassy eyes into the real world—our world—detached and apathetic, as though studying us. Her head and shoulders filled the picture, there was little room for any background, any context. Yet, something was missing.

I left her on the easel and slept almost twenty-four hours, a black, dreamless sleep. When I woke, I was inspired. I grabbed all my blues and drew long, meandering strokes, a mélange of cobalt and cerulean and ultramarine. I swept watered-down acrylic across her pallid cheeks and chiseled eyes so she appeared submerged, and with a flick of my brush her hair floated under the water. Drowning but not; gazing into the room with fortitude and composure. Defying her own mortality.

I tumble when I look at her. I dive into the ocean. And float. And sink. I'm caught in her lifeless eyes, lured toward her. One step, another. My feet sink into deep sand and languid waves crumple against the shore. The voices in the room are the tide, sweeping and swirling onto themselves, rhythmic and soporific. A salty breeze brushes my face and rests on my lips. The sky is clear, and miles of ocean stretch to the sharp indigo horizon.

"Jo."

The floor and walls build themselves around me. The

waves are voices once more. The air is stagnant with a mild odor of alcohol and sweat.

"Jo, Lily's here." He places his hands on my shoulders and points me in her direction.

TWO

B esides Nathan, Lily is my only friend, and she continually surprises me with her patience and kindness. I watch as she and her husband dutifully accept the brochure and glass of wine they're offered at the door and pause to scan the room for me. Nathan waves, which is what I should have done.

"Congratulations," Daniel says, bending to kiss my cheek.

"This is incredible, I'm so proud of you." Lily pulls me into a one-arm embrace and does a little glee-filled jig on the spot. "How's it going?"

"Good, I guess." I crane my neck to peer between torsos, to check enthusiasm levels and eavesdrop on nearby conversations.

Guests move slowly around, adhering to the accepted flow; several consult their catalogues and point out pieces to each other while also debating whether they'll make their dinner reservation on time. One or two are alone, pausing for several minutes in front of a piece with their arms folded and heads titled in consideration—"serious buyers," Lily stage-whispers with a wink, and I stare at them gracelessly.

A few are already heading for the exit, and I want to rush over and usher them back inside. I bounce on my toes until Nathan holds me down with an effortless hand on my shoulder.

"I can't believe I'm this nervous. Is it normal?"

"Yes, of course it is. You need a drink." Lily scurries to the table by the door and returns with two glasses of white.

Nathan's pointing to *On the Beach at Twilight*. He's telling Daniel about the tiny mark he made when the paint was drying. "I threw a tangerine at Jo, and she missed," he'll be saying, trying to contain his mirth. He didn't laugh when I chucked it back and hit his ear, leaving sticky juice trailing down his neck.

The hubbub ripples around us—low voices and indistinct conversations. Somewhere, the gallery owner is mingling and when she spots me, shielded by friends, she'll expect me to do the same. I stare at the jumble of faces and my heart palpitates.

Lily nudges my arm. "Smile. You're supposed to be enjoying yourself."

"Have you seen anyone buying anything? I don't think anyone's—"

"It's the opening night. These people are here by invitation because they'll get good press coverage, not because they'll necessarily buy everything today. You *know* that."

She works in marketing, handling events like this for her own clients all the time. Sometimes she gives me tickets when the numbers are low, so I *do* know. These guests are prominent art patrons and critics and minor celebrities who've just returned from a house or talent show or jungle. They waft past the paintings, more interested in their own careers than mine.

"I could be at home, reading a book ..." I mutter.

"Stop being a grouch, or I won't let you have any more wine," Lily hisses with a twinkle in her eye. She nods toward a bejeweled lady in a floral brocade jacket. "Her. Go and talk to her." And she propels me across the floor.

I stand awkwardly beside the stern, austere woman who

reminds me of a headmistress or librarian. "Hello," I say as Nathan and Lily gesture fervently. "I'm Jo Mckye. The artist," I add as she folds her arms and surveys me with derision.

"Ah, the artist. I see."

I wait for more, but she purses her lips.

"This is *Goddess in Pink*," I say, as if introducing two people at a dinner party.

"Yes, I read the card."

In this picture, Zenna is walking across a field of bright yellow rapeseed, wearing a pale pink dress—Potter's Pink, the tube said. She's facing into the picture, slightly turned toward us, as though her attention is caught by something unexpected in the room. It almost makes me turn to look.

"I prefer the one over there." She points limply to *In Grief* in the corner but doesn't seem altogether interested in any of them. "It has ..." She flourishes her hand in lieu of any actual opinion.

"Thank you."

"Is it a self-portrait?"

"No."

"I see." She pauses as though she's going to say something more, and then edges away, leaving me alone.

Zenna in the Sea, across the room, winks at me. An icy draught spirals around me, and I'm lifted from the floor, floating inches above the heads of everyone else. The noise of the room is muffled as though I'm under water alongside Zenna.

"She's a bit of an obsession, isn't she?"

The room jolts. I land with a thud, and everything is normal again. Lily and Daniel are talking to another couple, Nathan is loitering by the small table of hors d'oeuvres, and the general vibe is refined but charitable. The interloper grins expectantly, and I smile politely.

"She's the focus of the exhibition; I wouldn't call her an obsession." Except, I would. She is. I can't extract myself from her grasp.

"I've still got the postcard you drew for me. It's the same woman, isn't it?"

"I—" I gawp; my heart quickens. Someone from *before*, but I have no idea who. I take in his graying temples, the worn collar of his shirt, the sheen of sweat across his forehead. One of my uni lecturers, perhaps, come to check up on his star student. Or an old boyfriend from whom I parted when his intentions veered dramatically from mine.

He laughs self-consciously. "I haven't changed that much, have I?"

"No, of course not." I swallow my puzzlement. "It's lovely to see you again."

"Is that all?"

"Um ..."

"Jo?" His easy smile gives way to confusion.

"I'm sorry, I ... I don't remember ..."

He takes a step away from me.

"No, don't. It's not you. My memory ..." I never explain it properly. I avoid people so I don't have to. "I've lost a few years here and there." I grope for the right word. "Amnesia."

Such a small word; it never feels enough. My memories from the last three years are sharp and clear; beyond that, I have nothing but vague emotions and the odd incident which spikes through.

"Amnesia? So, you don't remember anything about me, university?"

I shrug apologetically. "Small things, unimportant things."

"Oh."

"No! I didn't mean *you* were unimportant. I meant ..." I wave my hands and flounder, wishing I had never come to this stupid place.

"I'm not sure what to say now." He surveys me, as if to catch me out in my lie. "Well, okay … I'm Spencer. We were at university together. We—um—were friends." He raises his eyebrows with a glint and a leisurely smirk.

"Right." I nod in mortification and discomfort; my cheeks burn.

In the silence growing around us, we both turn to the wall and stare at all the Zennas lined up. Red stickers have appeared beside some of the pieces. I overhear a meticulous discussion about *Sunrise*—which is a far simpler piece than their convoluted opinions are making out.

"She's different," Spencer says with profound consideration. "She wasn't so sinister or severe before." He sips his wine, swilling it around the glass, and wanders across to *Sunrise* as the other group moves away.

I'm not used to people taking my work so seriously. It's so far from my intent when I put the canvas on the easel or select watercolors over acrylic. Apparently, even the tiniest stroke has deep meaning.

My wine is warm; I've held it too long. "I should really—"

"You're scared of her, aren't you?"

"Of course not. She's just a painting." My fake, bright smile falters for a second. Because she's not. I hide my frown in the wineglass and collect myself. "Are you a critic, or something?"

"A journalist these days, actually—is it that obvious? I was never going to make it in the art world. I never had the talent you did." He reaches into his jacket pocket and offers a business card. "I'd love to interview you. I think you'd be fascinating." *Fascinating* remains on his lips for a second.

"Oh, I don't really … I'm not good at talking about myself." I force myself to pause and take a breath, to be more coherent. "I mean, I prefer to let my work speak for itself."

"You realize that's a cop-out?"

He's close, suddenly. Or, suddenly, I'm aware of it. He's tall; my eyes are level with the curve of his neck. I breathe the scent of his aftershave. I take a step back to retain the space between us, aware of my escalating pulse.

In the middle of the room, Nathan's in conversation with the woman I spoke to earlier—or at least, she's in conversation while he nods with wide-eyed mystification. He mouths: *Okay?* I nod: *You?* He rolls his eyes and downs his half-full glass. Lily's taking photos, gathering people and arranging their pose. She catches my eye and swishes through the small groups toward us.

"Say cheese," she says, and we do. "For Twitter," she explains, focused on the screen and tapping out a few words. "Hashtag *Jo Mckye*," she calls over her shoulder as she moves back into the throng.

We've lost the flow of the conversation, of whatever was going to happen. We giggle with embarrassment.

"Well," he says. "I should let you mingle. It's been great catching up. I'll be in touch about the interview—I mean it." His eyes narrow. "You *really* don't remember me? It's not a cheap line to avoid me?"

I shake my head. "I really don't, I'm sorry."

"Uh ..." He raises his glass to me and walks away with a wry smile.

THREE

O n my way to work the path is littered with crisp red and golden leaves. I crunch them underfoot, deliberately lurching toward the curb to kick through the deepest piles, childishly satisfied.

Dressed in my barista uniform, I'm anonymous again—the veneration and euphoria of the last few days has expired, the anti-climax sits heavily on my chest. Commuters driving past have no idea my art is hanging on the walls of a gallery. Pedestrians overtaking my slow dawdle won't care people have paid to own it. I want to stop everyone and tell them. I want to jump up and down and yell *Look at me!*

I pull my bobble hat further down my forehead and wedge my scarf into the neck of my coat. At the café, a surge of warmth from the overhead heater sends a welcome shiver down my spine.

Phil, the manager, is already here, turning on the coffee machine, filling the till with float money. Rafael follows me in. We make jovial small-talk as we busy ourselves with the other start-of-day tasks. I allow their banter to wash over me, saying as little as possible. Given the choice, I wouldn't socialize at all. I'd be a recluse, secreted away at home and churning out paintings. I'd work for days and nights on end, lost in a creative miasma, emerging randomly to eat or crash into bed.

Nathan and Lily are fundamental in this utopia. I couldn't live without them. They make sense of me; they know my history better than I do. When terror strikes in the middle of the night and I forget where I am, they hold my hand until I'm calm again. In my hermitism, they'd provide conversation and solace.

The hours at work are sluggish. The dreary and sustained rain is keeping people away. Those who do appear explode into the room to snatch a brief respite from the freezing drizzle —wrapping cold hands around their hot chocolate and making it last much longer than it ought.

"Good morning, Jo," says a familiar voice. Bridget, a chaotic sixty-something with frizzy black hair and a Smoked Purple lipstick smile is at the counter in front of me.

"Hi! How was your holiday?" I pass a takeaway cup to a waiting customer and turn to her with a grin to mirror hers.

"Amazing. Everything I hoped. I did absolutely *everything*. I've got so many photos, you wouldn't believe."

I set a tray on the counter for her order and turn to prepare her usual flat white. She asks for a Victoria sponge and sits at her favorite table by the window, gazing absently at the walls.

Last year, after working here for a few weeks, I let slip I was an artist and Phil swapped his generic poster art for a few of my pieces. He thought it would garner business for us both. I'm not sure how much it's succeeded—occasionally customers glance at them while eating, but mostly they blend into the background. Despite the price tags, a lot of people don't realize they're for sale.

Bridget bought a couple, which is how we started talking. I'm never certain she genuinely liked them, or if she was just being altruistic.

I deliver her coffee and cake and slide into the seat opposite, taking advantage of the next lull. "How does it feel to be back? How long was it—six weeks?"

"Just over. It's pretty dull, actually. On holiday, every day was different and exciting. I'd get up in the morning and make spontaneous decisions. I never knew what would happen next—it was fantastic." She pushes her fork into the sponge and strawberry jam oozes from the sides. "You know what I came back to? Two letters from the hospital and a gas bill." She laughs grimly and savors the cake.

I squirm. How can she make jokes about it?

"Over there, no one knew I was ill—no one needed to. I was just the mad English woman. Back here, I'm the cancer patient, the next name on the list. No, that's not fair—my doctor's great." Her eyes focus on a couple rushing past the window, coats pulled over their heads. "Perhaps I should go away again and not come back ..." She slaps the table, pushing away her dejection. "Anyway, how are you? Oh"—she pats my arm excitedly—"I saw your exhibition yesterday. Stunning. Really stunning. Such a magical creature you created."

As always, she doesn't give me time to linger on her sadness. I'm grateful; conversations like this discomfit me—I never know if I'm doing or saying the right thing. She said the same about me, once. She said she felt guilty when she spoke of her past because I didn't have one. She asked if I ever felt isolated, if anxiety kept me awake at night.

"*In Grief* was my favorite," she says. "But it was already sold when I saw it. It felt a lot more intimate than your usual work. I could sense your love pouring from the canvas."

"She's just a character. No one I know." I fuss with her spare napkin, folding down the corners and smoothing them into sharp edges.

Bridget says love; Spencer said fear. How interesting people isolate such conflicting concepts. Neither is correct—they're too precise, too final. I painted Zenna with reflection and sadness and curiosity. I searched for her vulnerabilities, for her story—but even now, at the end of it all, she's elusive.

"Really? I'm surprised." Bridget ponders for a moment, taking another forkful of cake. "You've painted her with such understanding and humanity. Perhaps she's someone you once knew?"

A little girl giggles—it diverts me for a moment. I glance around, but the only child in the café is asleep in her buggy.

"What are you still doing here, Jo?"

"Sorry?" What was it she said, about knowing Zenna? I try to grasp the thread of her conversation, but it unravels.

"You're wasted here. I mean, you make good coffee and all, but you're an *artist*. Look at your exhibition, at these paintings right here"—with a sweep of her hand in the air—"they're special. *You're* special. You should be experiencing the world, mixing with artists in Paris and Venice, drinking Champagne in the middle of the afternoon. I'm serious, you should be hanging in the Tate and the Guggenheim." She nods in agreement with herself. "Trust me, time goes far too quickly."

I squeeze her hand and return to the counter, catching the fleeting melancholy in her eyes. She stares at the picture in front of her—my watercolor of a hand reaching for a coffee cup. In the background, I painted a window facing out onto an ocean. There are no faces, no emotion, yet several people say they find it sad—a woman sitting alone. They suppose she's waiting for someone, or it's a comment on unrequited love—and they share their own sad stories with me while I squirm and search for an escape.

"Why did you paint a window?" one woman asked, overlooking the jilted hand. "If I was that close to the ocean, I'd be outside with the surf on my face and the sun warming my skin. What does the window represent?"

Bridget subconsciously mimics the position of the painted hand as she drains her cup. I want to hug her, to save her. But while I serve my next customer, she heads to the door with an affable wave.

FOUR

S pencer called to arrange my interview. Damn.

"Hey, remember me?"

"Of course."

"I wasn't sure, with the whole memory thing."

"Long term, not short term."

"Right. Cool. Are you free tomorrow, about eleven?"

My shoulders drooped and I grimaced into the mirror I was stood in front of. I scratched black paint off my nose. "Sure," I said with a smile.

Now, outside the coffee shop where we agreed to meet, I'm nervous. My hand shakes as I push the door open and I steel myself with a deep breath. It's quiet, only a few people dotted around, working on laptops or reading newspapers. Spencer's sitting in the dimly lit far corner; he rises from his chair and meets me at the counter.

He lines up to buy me a drink, and I sit at the table to compose myself. I try to picture our younger selves together. He's tall and slim, with curly hair reminiscent of Cumberbatch as Sherlock—I had good taste in men, back then. I wonder how his arms would have felt sweeping me into an embrace. When Nathan, more muscular and a little shorter, hugs me I'm safe and content. Spencer would rouse excitement and danger. Ruffled, I cough to conceal the soft smile playing on my lips.

My fingers comb through my hair and snag on a clump of dried paint which I flick onto the floor. I remove my jacket and billow my shirt to allow air to flow around me. I wipe my hands across my face and imagine the city grime clinging to me. I'll never get used to the weight of polluted air pushing me down.

"So." Spencer returns and organizes the mugs, moving them off the tray along with the napkins and spoons. He slides the tray onto a neighboring table. "It's so good to see you again."

So good? I try to gather clues. What was I like when he knew me? Have I changed? Did he love me? It won't do any good to ask out right—people with memories filter them, edit them. They possess whimsical versions of themselves and their past.

"You too."

"Even though you don't know who I am?"

I blush. "Yeah, even then."

"How does it work? Are there things you remember? Is it permanent? Does it come and go?"

Too many questions. With each one he inches closer to me across the table. I press myself into the back of my chair and, after a moment, he relaxes into his.

"It is what it is. I don't know how to describe it. I mean, how would you describe living with your past constantly rattling around in your head? Don't you feel full up? Is *everyone* you've ever met locked up inside you?"

He grins. "Fair enough. Daft question."

"Sorry, I didn't mean—"

"No, I get it. It's okay." He clicks his pen against the table—on, off, on, off—and repositions his mobile so it's directly between us.

"I don't usually talk about my condition. People tend to back off pretty sharpish when they discover I'm not normal."

"Normal is overrated. Shall we get started?" He moves seamlessly into interview mode—the breezy persona who'll narrate the article. "So, your first solo exhibition? How does it feel? You must be pretty excited?"

"Oh yes. It's been a lot of work, but I'm so happy." I recount the Instagram story of being discovered.

"Is that a typical way to be approached?" he asks, in a tone suggesting he knows it's not.

"No. I guess I was in the right place at the right time. Or, at least, my painting was."

I'd always assumed the gallery owner was a friend of Nathan's who owed him a favor—or he *asked* for a favor. But at the opening, there was no specific intimacy between them. They barely acknowledged each other. I ought to ask; I ought to know.

"Your exhibition features one woman—Zenna. Tell me about her."

"Well, she's an accident, I suppose. Or at least the way she came about is. I was trying to paint a self-portrait. But Zenna appeared on the canvas instead. The next time I picked up my brush, I didn't really have a plan, and she came back. With something like *On the Beach in Twilight*, she's in the background, but she's still there."

"At what point did you decide to place her at the heart of the show?"

"When I painted *Zenna in the Sea*. She had a story, and I needed to discover what it was."

"Did you find it?"

"It's ... evolving."

"You used to draw her before, at uni."

"You said that the other night." It must mean something—being followed from one existence to another by the same creation?

"Do you think she's someone from your past, someone important?"

University was over a decade ago; I only lost my memory three years ago. It doesn't make sense I'd be preoccupied by the same character at such different points in my life.

"The collection is about vulnerability and hidden strength. Reality and fantasy merging together." I'm waffling, wasting words. I wish this was over. I sip my coffee and peer at the large clock above the counter.

Spencer's pen hovers over his notebook. "That sounds like something Jim Turner would have said. One of our lecturers," he prompts when I don't respond.

I smile tightly. "Oh right. Well, maybe I remember more than I think I do."

"Did you always want to be an artist?" he reads from his notebook.

"I ... guess so."

His eyes widen. "Shit, sorry. Insensitive question. I didn't mean to—"

"It's okay. It's a memoryful world—people take it for granted.

"It can't be easy." He flicks his pen between his fingers and rests his hand on his cup as if he's going to pick it up but doesn't. "Aren't you ever curious? Don't you want to know more about yourself?"

Yes ... No ... It wouldn't do me any good ... Of course, I do ... Where would I even begin?

I exist with chunks of myself veiled in fog, a vague blur in my peripheral vision, a ghost. Other people have the comfort of reminiscing or basing choices off previous experiences; but each of my days is brand new. No reflections or portents, no moments of delight when a casual recollection is evoked. I'm trapped in an interminable present.

It's impossible to explain, especially to a casual acquaintance in a coffee shop. As my stumbling silence continues, Spencer reads through his notes again, flipping the page to censor his prepared questions.

"What's your workspace like?"

"I paint in my bedroom, at the moment. I'd love a studio, but I can't afford one. My bed's pushed into one corner, my clothes are on a rack, and I have to climb over stacked canvases and boxes of paints to reach the window." I glance at my crumpled, paint-flecked shirt, and shrug. I don't need to explain—it's obvious I'm living as a vagabond.

He follows my eyes and smiles warmly. "You were never one for dressing up. You'd turn up at uni parties just like this—you wore dungarees a lot."

"Lots of pockets," I say automatically.

"Yep, that's what you said back then." He laughs. "You didn't care what people thought. It's one of the things I ... liked about you."

His expression softens, but I blush with shame. *This* is his memory of me? Scatty and unkempt?

What happened between us? I'm longing to ask. But what if he tells me it was my fault? What if we fought and cried in despair and had months of make-up sex which did nothing but cause more misery? Time will have soothed his memory, but my probing could shake it all up again. I have to accept he knows more than me—it's not the first time.

"We'll probably use one of the publicity photos from the gallery." He winks and I cover my face with my hand.

"I got caught up," I mumble through my fingers. "I was running late."

"I was joking."

"It's been a while since I've—" What? Met up with people other than Lily or Nathan, been on a date? What exactly am I going to say next?

Crockery clatters across the room and we both start, jumping in our seats, saving me from finishing my sentence. I drink. Spencer coughs and glances toward the window.

"Why art?"

"Sorry?"

He gestures to his notebook. Of course, the interview.

"You already asked. I don't remember."

"No, I mean ... you're always an artist. You studied art, you had work featured in student shows and afterwards"— I raise my eyebrows, and he nods in confirmation—"and without any memory of your previous life, you return to painting."

"Uh, that's a good point." How can I still be so shocked by these things I don't know? "But I couldn't imagine doing anything else. I don't always feel part of the world, I don't understand it. But when I paint, everything's a lot clearer."

Spencer scribbles in his book and glances at his mobile to check the recording time.

I drain my cup. He's obviously disappointed with who I am now—this empty shell I've become. *Were we in love?* I bite my tongue to prevent myself asking.

"What's next? Are you working on anything new?"

"I'm trying out a more abstract style at the moment." *Zenna, I'm still painting Zenna and I can't stop.*

"Another departure?"

"I like the challenge."

The tables around us are filling up. I'm struck by a couple sitting opposite each other with unyielding intensity, holding hands almost to the point of aggression. Two men— one with tears in his eyes, the other leaning forward, whispering urgently. The end of a relationship or the amplifying of an existing one. The second man's hand is on top, gripping tightly, afraid perhaps to let go.

On canvas, I'd identify their story immediately. I glance

at my bag where my sketchpad awaits me. My fingers fiddle with the napkin, itching for a pencil.

Spencer pushes his notebook to the middle of the table. "I had a whole heap of questions about your childhood, your influences, your plans. I guess none of them are relevant."

"I have plans!" I sit up straight in my indignation.

"Go on."

And I pause, because I don't have plans. My only hope for the future is everything will remain the same, that my current memories won't start to slip away too. With no past, the future seems unimportant. "It doesn't matter."

"So, I guess that's it. I think I've got what I need." He leans back in his chair with a sigh. "To be honest, I was hoping to make this last a little longer ... until dinner, maybe?"

I smile with regret. "You seem ... you *are* a nice bloke, but you've seen how broken I am. It's easier for me to stay away from entanglement."

"Entanglement?"

"I didn't mean—" I blush again, furious heat overtaking my whole face.

He laughs, hiding a flash of irritation, perhaps. He's hard to read, shifting from professional to flirtatious and back without me catching it. "I think it would have been fun, if we'd managed to stick together all those years ago, don't you?"

"I'm sorry." I shrug because I don't know.

He gathers his things, dropping them into the rucksack under the table. "I'll text you when the article's published." He pushes his chair into the gap behind him. "You've got my card—give me a call if you fancy a drink, or a chat, or ..." He leans to kiss my cheek and walks away with a whistle.

FIVE

I'm cross-legged on the floor in front of the large mirror I've dragged from the hall and propped against the wall. I light a candle to my right which softens my features with a warm orange glow.

When I first painted Zenna, I'd been trying for a self-portrait. Telling Spencer has made me want to try again.

It's past midnight. The main light's off, so the corners of the room are masked and eerie. I focus on my reflection—every shadow, every line and blemish, until my face becomes alien, until I can view myself with the same indifference I casually study customers in the café, or the anonymous mass of commuters who swarm alongside me each evening.

Charcoal skims across the page, a proliferation of lines. I blow away black dust to reveal the outline of my face. I examine myself again—scooping hair away from my jaw and tilting my head so the candlelight dances on my skin. It creates the illusion of myself in motion.

Once my features are sketched out, I select the Flesh Ochre pastel and layer it over the charcoal, emphasizing my cheekbones and nose, adding depth and contour. For contrast, I smudge Carmine on my lips and Van Dyke Brown on my eyes. Those flashes of color are striking against the black and white.

I hold it into the light. And it's not me.

Zenna. Again. Still.

But today, I'm not affronted by her presence—I welcome her. It's fitting she's here, although I can't pinpoint why. As I gaze at her, I'm absorbed into her world. I'm floating, bobbing on water with waves lapping over me and the horizon tipping from side to side. She's beside me to prevent me slipping beneath the water, and I'm safe in her arms. Slowly, her presence wanes and I'm alone, empty and disoriented. She's pressed back onto the page.

I unfold myself and go into the kitchen in search of chocolate cake. I cut a huge slice and sit at the table, facing the window. We're on the first floor of a two-story building, so I peer down on the unnerving and forsaken road below. I sketch ghosts into the silhouettes, and they wander the length of the street, their eerie faces captured in the streetlights.

The light right outside shines into the room, streaking the walls with orange. The candle's burning faintly. In the flames, Zenna's half-turned toward me with her hand held out. *Come*, she says, and I reach for her. But she's too far ahead, and I'm running on soft, damp sand to catch up. My feet sink, and I can't scramble out of the ditches my steps have created.

I eat cake with one hand and draw Zenna with the other.

***

My limbs are frozen and sore. The candle burned out hours ago and the heating is always off overnight. I'm curled against the arm of the sofa, my portrait of Zenna propped against the opposite wall. I've been awake all night, unable to sleep.

Remember.

"Nathe?"

Remember me. You have to find me. You have to remember.

"Jo, wake up, you're having a bad dream." Nathan shakes me, rousing me. "You were screaming."

My limbs are frozen and sore. I'm lying on the sofa, my arms tucked under me in search of warmth; the candle burned out hours ago. I stretch out and gasp as pain pulses through my shoulder. The portrait of Zenna is propped against the wall.

I'm groggy when I shower. Each movement is labored and taxing, and I dress with equal difficulty. I'm going to be late meeting Lily for breakfast but rushing only slows me down as I make ham-fisted mistakes.

Whereas I have a vague understanding of how I met Nathan, I don't recall meeting Lily at all—she's always just been there. She refers to events and conversations as though we've shared them, and then explains I was indeed present. In larger groups, she whispers pertinent facts about our shared acquaintances. It must be tedious for her, to recap the same things time and again, but she always smiles, never avoids certain subjects because of it.

I emerge from the Marble Arch tube station into warm, bright sunshine. The evergreens along the boundary of Hyde Park are radiant; the sky is French Ultramarine, with flat, feathery clouds.

This whole end of Oxford Street is a hub of tourist activity, visitors and locals all mixed up together. People brush against me as though I'm invisible.

Remember ... Remember me.

I shiver despite the heat. The ground shifts beneath me, unbalancing me. No one else is affected; they pass by as easily as they did a moment ago. I lean against a paint-peeling door and close my eyes. Dizziness rises and passes in an instant. I search for the voice, for someone whispering in my ear, but no one's paying attention to me, lost in their own early morning contemplations.

By the time I reach Lily, everything has returned to normal. No voices, no quake beneath my feet—just a residue of exhaustion and disquiet.

We battle the belligerent stream of traffic and the lights which control it, and head into Hyde Park. Almost immediately, London vanishes. Wind rustles through trees tall enough to obscure the buildings over toward Westminster. Only the highest towers peek over the tops. I filter out the car horns and roar of motorcycles; I ignore the sirens and drone of engines.

Lily says I've always loved this park. Early in our friendship, I told her I felt trapped by the long Regency terraces and suffocated by the heat deflected off them. I talked about sea breezes, she says, as though they were an elixir.

"You're not yourself today." Lily directs me to the left as our path converges with another, guiding me toward the Serpentine.

"Just tired. I was up all night. I think the adrenaline of the exhibition has evaporated."

"It's a lot of work," she agrees. "Nathan mentioned you were having nightmares?"

"He fusses too much." I kick through a line of crispy russet leaves.

"He cares about you, worries about you. We both do."

"There's a woman at work—a customer. She says I should leave, go traveling." I'm surprised I've mentioned it; it didn't seem important at the time.

"Where?"

"Anywhere, I guess. She said I'm wasting my time here, that I should focus on painting and have adventures."

Lily tips her head from side to side, weighing her response. "Will you?"

The park is bustling this morning. A mother and toddler are at the water, throwing food for the ducks. On the other side of the lake, tourists are gathered at the memorial fountain. The whole place is full of people jogging or dog-walking, businesspeople in suits and trainers speed-walking to their next appointment, and students reading or lounging.

"*Why* would I leave? Look at this, it's beautiful." I spread my arms out to embrace the view. "All these people have chosen to come here, from all over the world, for holidays or to live here, because it's amazing. And I'm already here. I don't need to be anywhere else."

"You're right. I sometimes forget that."

At the kiosk, Lily orders coffee and two large blueberry muffins, which she claims are kind of breakfast. I stand on the bank of the Serpentine while the order is filled. Several canoes glide past; a duck flaps its wings excitedly. Every couple of minutes, a plane descends toward Heathrow, stalking across the sky.

In truth, London's all I know, familiar and safe. I can navigate the Tube and feel at home in the anonymous surge of people. If I left, I'd probably go to Australia or Japan, where the way of life is so different than here. Even a coffee shop job in Melbourne sounds exotic after trudging back and forth in dark British winters, year after year.

Other people might return to their hometown, I suppose. They'd return to the comfort of their roots, to reset themselves for the next stage of their life. But *home* is an undefined idea for me—a vague rendering. Small recollections push through my subconscious, but they're stifled almost immediately.

"Have you ever lived anywhere else?" I take my cup and muffin from Lily and we sit on the grass.

"I went to university in Sheffield, but I came back straight after. Daniel was here, and we were already engaged. He had a good job, so it was sensible." She instinctively strokes the rings on her finger, the engagement and wedding rings designed to be entwined. "We might move one day, but not yet."

I pull the muffin into two pieces, biting into the bottom half and saving the top for last—it's where the fruit has congregated and sugar has been sprinkled.

We're the same age, Lily and I, and yet she's married, settled, happy. They're planning to start a family, to be responsible for a whole new human being. Mid-thirties, and I'm alone—I guess it's my fate. How would a relationship even work? Will my amnesia get worse? Will I wake one morning and forget today?

"Bridget, the woman at work, is amazing though. She lives each day—"

"—like it's her last?" Lily says, rolling her eyes.

"No," I say with a soft smile, picturing Bridget's enthusiasm when she was telling me about her trip. "Like it's her first." Like I have to.

SIX

The weather turns. Rain trickles down the window and the café is gloomy yet snug. Only yesterday I was sitting in the park with Lily, and today I want to hibernate within these walls—to curl up and hide away. I go through the motions of working, slow and labored, lacking the momentum to keep moving. Sometimes I stop altogether, stock still in the middle of the room as if I've forgotten where I am.

Phil watches while I allow Kate and Rafael to cover for me, gathering up the customers I fail to acknowledge.

"Oi," Phil says, ducking in front of me to attract my attention. "What's up?"

"Nothing."

"Look, I know your art stuff is taking off—and that's great—but whatever's happening in your own time, I need you to be focused when you're here. Got it?"

I nod, chastised like a schoolchild, and he walks back to the small kitchen. Rafael smiles as he wipes down the tables I should be doing. I can't decide if he's sympathizing or laughing at me, so I half-smile in return and tidy some chairs.

My shift inches along. The orders and people merge into one another. The world speeds up; I slow down. Today, the whispering is a sea breeze that swirls around me melodically.

"Hi, how can I help?... No, but this lemon cake is gluten free ... Hi, what can I get you?... Take a seat, I'll bring it right over ... Hi, what would you like this morning?... Do you want marshmallows with the hot chocolate?... Take a seat ... Hi ..."

Two women scan the board behind the counter. "What would you like, Mum?" asks the younger with her purse already in her hand.

"Just a pot of tea, love."

"And a cake?"

"Oh no, I couldn't possibly." The older woman pats her stomach self-consciously.

"We'll share. Half a muffin each?" And they peer at the gooey cakes on display.

The daughter catches my eye and smiles indulgently. "The double chocolate muffin, and a pot of tea for two, please."

I envy their easy discourse, their affection. "I'll bring it over."

They're huddled together when I take the order across, scrolling through photos on their mobiles, laughing at their expressions, at their failed effort at a selfie in front of Big Ben. As I set out the teapot and cups, they attempt another—cheeks squashed together as they lean to fit into the shot.

"You've got to look at the camera bit, not the screen," the daughter says through tears of mirth. She flashes their cross-eyed picture at me and shakes her head.

"Would you like me to take a photo for you?"

"Oh yes, thank you so much."

They pose, and I take several. With each click, transient yearnings for my own mother catch in my throat—to sit with her this way and share a cake, or to pop round and curl up on her sofa while we talk inconsequential nonsense.

It's a ridiculous thought—we haven't seen each other in

years, and I don't think of her often because I can't. I'm aware I have a mother, who cared for me and took me to school and cooked tea while I sat at the kitchen table with my homework—but I don't recall any of it. Not one single moment sticks in my head. She's as blank as the rest of my past. I don't even remember what she looks like.

"We don't get together often," the daughter explains, pulling me back into the room. "Mum lives in Margate and finds it hard to travel these days." She squeezes her mother's hand and wipes away a tear. "We should make the time. I should come to you more often."

Nathan says I mentioned Mum a few times, long ago, and assumed we'd argued. He's vague on details. It was my choice to leave, but simply walking away makes no sense. Why didn't I go back? What could possibly have happened so irreparable? I press my fingertips into my temples, trying to push the regrets back inside.

Here are some other things I've forgotten.

I've forgotten my friends. I follow people on Twitter (strangers), and people whose friend requests I've accepted on Facebook (who may or may not know me in real life, I'm not sure), but I have no sense of the history we've shared.

I've forgotten my GCSE results, and the presumed pressure of taking them.

I've forgotten my favorite actors and bands, and which TV shows were unmissable for me. I don't know what posters I had on my walls.

Once, Nathan spent a whole afternoon following YouTube links for the theme tunes of his favorite childhood programs. He was thrilled by how many he could still recall and sing along to.

"This one," he'd say, again and again, turning his laptop toward me. "*Willo the Wisp*, oh I loved that!"

Or: "Hey, *Button Moon?*" and point to the big yellow button in the sky and the wooden spoons traveling to it in their washing-up bottle spaceship.

Or: "*Rentaghost?* Everyone knows that one."

I peered at the screen, at the shaky camerawork and hand-drawn titles, dredging my brain for the smallest snippet of familiarity until it physically hurt.

He continued for hours, following every suggested link and circling back around to ones we'd already watched, until he discovered programs even he didn't recognize. I tried to rein in my irritation—it wasn't his fault, after all. It was *my* fault, my problem.

The mother and daughter stack their plates and pile several coins on the table as a tip. The scrape of chairs draws my attention back to them. "Thank you. Have a good afternoon."

They pause outside, sorting out their bags and coats. The mother says something, and her daughter hugs her tightly. I feel the hug, their arms enveloping me.

Remember.

Remember what? But there's no one nearby to ask.

***

Tonight, I'm buried alive. I'm in my bed, but a steep, compacted mud wall surrounds me, rising to the ceiling. From a small gap at the top, my parents weep. Imagined versions of them, silhouettes, glimmers.

I struggle and scream, but they're agitated in their grief and don't notice my frantic efforts to climb out. They throw soil on top of me. Zenna's beside them, gazing down with sorrow and pity. She throws the final handful which covers me completely.

Tangled in my bedding, I can't breathe. The earth fills my lungs.

And then I'm okay. I'm in my bed, and I'm not being buried. I'm still alive. Zenna's in her painting and my parents are far, far away.

Remember me.

It's not quite five o'clock—still dark, with the early chill frosting the air. I relax into my pillow and study the ceiling warily, to ensure no one's peering back. I go into the kitchen and make strong black coffee.

Rather than go back to bed, I take my mug and sketchbook into the main room, comforted by the notion everything is manageable once it's on paper, under my control. I ponder how to recreate the steep sides of the grave, how to convey the claustrophobia and haunting anguish of my own demise.

I close my eyes, conjuring the faces from my dream, conjuring Zenna.

Zenna. Fascinating yet ominous. Like the opening scene of a horror film where everything is normal and harmless, but you anticipate something terrible from the start because you've paid to be terrified.

Zenna was real, in the dream—she wasn't painted or sketched. Her flesh was warm, and blood pulsed through her.

My mother, in contrast, was the shadow, the fiction I couldn't bring to life. Her features undefined and tenuous. A remnant of my past, she fades out when I get too close. My father is less than that. While Mum remains in my thoughts, Dad disintegrates.

Nathan once told me he always thinks of his mother as being in her late thirties—there was a specific dress she wore, one particular family holiday, where she was so flawlessly *his*.

And it's a shock, he said, whenever he sees her, because she's almost seventy, and he forgets. He readjusts his perception of her each time. Yet he always reverts to his conviction of her enduring youth and vitality.

I can barely conceive my mother at all. I have a sense of her, but I can't picture her smile when she tucked me into bed or the ferocity of her temper when I was naughty or her various hairstyles and fashion choices over the years. If she or my dad walked past me in the street, I wouldn't recognize them. I'm not filled with warm sensations; I have no reference for such reactions.

I draw two oval placeholders, shaping their jaws and foreheads. Then I cross through one of them. The empty space fills me with unease.

SEVEN

On my bedroom wall, I have a mass of photos pinned up. Those I've taken myself and printed out; black-and-white studio portraits of Victorian ladies in their Sunday best bought from flea markets; several of me, acquired from forgotten sources. Snaps of my friends huddled in drunken clusters in dark nightclubs or lying on the grass on campus unaware photos were being taken.

Voices murmur, like a radio left on in another room—all these people, perhaps, telling me their stories. Are any of them my mother? Some of the pictures I think are me could be her. Perhaps we share a jawline or a sparkle in our eyes and as I age my features blur further into hers.

After so long without thinking about her, this onslaught of sentiment is disconcerting. The more I stare at the photos on the wall, the greater the weight of sadness. I tell people it doesn't bother me, not knowing where I came from—and for the most part it doesn't. Today, I want a hug from my mum.

"What are you doing?" Nathan asks, and I jump.

"Nothing. Just rummaging for inspiration." I unpin a selfie of the two of us. Nathan's arm is around my shoulder and we're pulling silly expressions into the camera. We're so young—our faces not fully lived in. "When was this?"

He glances briefly. "I didn't realize you had this one. It

was a few years ago, after uni, a day trip we took to ..." He shrugs indifferently. "Somewhere or other. I'm off now. See you later."

I take my sketchpad into the other room, curling up on the sofa and wrapping my fluffy blanket around me. I prefer it in here—there's more light and space. My room, with its dark mahogany furniture purchased cheaply from a house clearance, is stifling.

My hand drifts across the page, scratching lines and curves into the paper, shadowing and shading the face appearing in front of me. Always a face.

I'm scared to look properly, half-expecting it to be Zenna again. But this time, it's my mother—or at least, how I imagine her today. She's smiling enigmatically, with an elegance I'm not sure she ever possessed when I knew her. She's tender and loving in this version; she glows. She's a moment away from bending to kiss me goodnight, her necklace bumps against my cheek, her perfume fills the room.

I allow my eyes to close and feel her lips on my forehead. *Shhh,* she says softly, *time to go to sleep.* And I do, sliding into the darkness and dreaming about her.

Except, it's not *about* her; I *am* her, assimilated into her, stretching into her arms and legs, with her wooden bangles on my wrist and long skirt flapping at my ankles. My subconscious mind tries to escape, tries to position me beside her, outside of her, but I remain encased. I'm in a rusty brown Mini, with a cigarette nestled between my fingers, grunting along an A road in the heart of Cornwall, heading somewhere magical and mysterious. The road's empty so I speed up, flying down hills and bouncing over bumps. "I Want to Break Free" springs from the radio, and I sing along with venom and bitterness, each word hissing from our lips.

Every so often we take a drag and blow a stream of smoke out of the window. It calms us. The nicotine floods our system, and we allow ourself to smile. Our long hair tangles in front of our eyes, until we tie it loosely at the nape of our necks. We put on our Jackie O sunglasses and check our reflection in the rear-view mirror.

She smiles, but she isn't happy.

In the back seat, directly behind her, I'm thrown from side to side as she overtakes slower cars and skates around the sharp bends of the narrow, hedged roads. She's going much faster than Daddy does, but I'm afraid to tell her in case she shouts. She checks on me in the mirror every so often, her mouth set in a tight line.

Are we there yet? I crane my neck to watch the road whooshing away from us.

No, she growls, as though I've been asking the same thing repeatedly. *We're having an adventure. This is fun*, she adds, though she doesn't sound enthusiastic. She speeds up, faster and faster, like a rollercoaster, until I'm lifted off the seat with the momentum.

The road sweeps into a long, gentle bend and the sun, low in the sky, shines into the car, turning the interior golden. Or is it just my sepia-tinted memory, obscure footage captured on an old cine film, an aged postcard lodged in my mind?

I don't know if Mum ever smoked, or owned a brown Mini, or had hair long enough to tie back. I don't know if we ever went on an adventure. My childhood is cobbled together from anecdotes and photos of events I don't recall; other people's memories stolen and claimed as my own. The fog around it is viscous—the more I wade through it, the denser it becomes.

The sketchpad slides from my lap and I'm no longer in the backseat of the car. There's a moment of stillness before the wave of whispering resumes.

"What's this?" Nathan says, appearing beside me and picking the pad up.

"Shit! You scared me. Stop sneaking around."

"I wasn't. Have you been here all night?"

The curtains are open; a repeat of *Murder, She Wrote* is on the TV. "What time is it?"

"Morning time." He glances at my drawing. "It's you? You've finally broken the Zenna 'curse?'" He makes little quote marks in the air.

"I think it's my mum. It's probably nothing like her." I take the pad from him, and she's already morphing into Zenna. I throw it to the other end of the sofa.

"It's good."

"I was just playing around. Mum's in my head, at the moment."

"Mmm."

"I might pop down for a few days, for a visit." I frown with confusion. *Where did that come from?* I'm sure it's *not* what I was going to say.

Once more, Zenna's walking across smooth white sand. Not a beach, an infinite desert. *Come with me.* I hold my hand out to her, desperate for her to grasp it and pull me toward her, but she maintains the same elusive distance. *I'm lost, Jo-Jo. I need you.*

Back in the room, I shiver and pull the blanket around my shoulders. Nathan's talking. I try to untangle his words.

"—didn't realize you kept in touch with her."

"What? No, I don't. It's been a while. I don't think we ... I guess we drifted apart?"

I unfurl myself and go to the kitchen. Nathan follows.

"How long?" he asks. "Since you saw her?"

"A long time. It's not important. Have we still got cheese-cake?"

"For breakfast? Top shelf." And he's already got a fork in his hand for me.

"Has anyone ever told you you're the perfect flatmate?"

"Well, I've only ever lived with you, so no."

I turn, mid-mouthful. "Really? How come?"

He pauses. "I lived with my parents, then alone."

"So, how come we live together now?"

"You ... had nowhere else to go."

"But I've been here for years, right?" I gulp my mouthful quickly, almost choking on the next question. "Was I supposed to move out?"

"No! Definitely not. It's been working well. I wouldn't have been able to afford this place by myself. You don't *want* to move out, do you?"

I shake my head. I can't begin to imagine a world without Nathan in it.

"Good."

In the other room, I retrieve the picture of my mother, who became Zenna, and reverted back to my mother. Should I visit? Is it what I really want? Would it help? I slide my finger across my plate, scooping up the last of the cheesecake crumbs.

Remember me.

EIGHT

At work, I stifle yawns, smothered by the inertia of another restless night. The voice is becoming a river of white noise. Random words picked out like blood-red drops on a canvas. Lucid and strident before fading back into an incoherent hum.

Remember me.

People come and go, cakes and cups balanced in their arms as they wrestle with the door. Or with trays and toddlers as they search for a table.

I'm lost.

The coffee machine hisses, glasses crash together in their basket, spoons clatter against the sides of mugs.

You have to find me.

As I clear tables, the lights flicker and a shadow crosses my path, pushing me off-balance as though someone's sprinting past and I'm caught in the slipstream. My throat is constricted, like hands are squeezing around me. I steady myself with the nearest table, gulping air.

"You all right, Jo?" Rafael calls. He's muffled, distant.

"Just dizzy."

I'm floundering underwater. Disorientated as if I've dived in and can't find my way to the surface. Ducking under, unable to break through. Not swimming, drowning. I taste saltwater. Swallow it.

My legs buckle and Raf's arms are holding me up, guiding me to a chair. I slump forward and close my eyes to stop the world from tumbling around me.

"I'm fine." The dizziness intensifies. I try to stand; my legs are jelly beneath me. I groan involuntarily.

I can't find you.

"Stay there," Phil orders, his hand resting on my shoulder to keep me from moving. He puts a glass of water into my hand. "Drink this. Any better?"

Remember me.

"I don't want to," I murmur, shaking my head, shaking the voice *out of* my head.

"Just a sip. I think we should get you to A&E."

"No, no I'll be all right in a minute. I'll sit here, I'll be fine." I raise my head, but it takes a while for the room to catch up. Everything around me is swirling, like Van Gogh's *Starry Night*. "Maybe it's a migraine?"

"I'll get Raf to drive you home."

"Don't go to any trouble. I'll get a taxi. I just want to lie down." I want to be sick. I want to stop drowning.

Hushed conversations take place above my head. Phil and Raf debate the taxi idea; some of the customers have congregated with curiosity or concern. I'm vaguely aware of the taxi being called, new customers entering and demanding service, the taxi arriving. Phil helps me to the car and I'm home in minutes. I crawl up the stairs, unable to walk erect without falling into the wall. I fumble my key into the lock.

"I'm home," I call out pathetically, without reply—Nathan's out just when I need him here.

I grope along the wall to my room and clamber onto the bed. It shifts and tilts and turns, buffeting me around. I cling to the mattress, searching for stability. Gradually, the giddiness and nausea begin to dissipate.

A persistent bird tweets outside my window—a discordant, irritating noise. Across the road, someone's receiving a delivery—the drivers are yelling instructions to each other, the item is large and weighty. In contrast, the hum of planes flying out of Heathrow is almost soothing, and the voice in my head is reassuring.

My mother screams. Blood-chilling and anguished.

I'm straight as a plank, my heart pounding into my stomach, holding my breath. But the flat's still empty. Nathan's at work, Mum's hundreds of miles away. The voice is a calming melody. *Shhh*, it says, as though soothing a baby. Am I the baby? Is this my mother trying to reach me? Is she in danger?

A stupid thought. She'd have called. Someone would have.

The dizziness returns. I clutch my skull until it ebbs to a mild fuzziness, as though I've had one too many glasses of wine yet am still on the right side of inebriation. I lie back onto my pillow and reach for the TV remote, skipping through the channels, barely conscious of the programs flicking past me.

It's not quite three o'clock, but already getting dark as clouds cloak the sky and spots of rain patter against the window. The room is gloomy and cold. I slide beneath my duvet.

Before she screamed, Mum was running toward me, terrified. There was no location, no backdrop—we weren't anywhere. We were inside a white bubble, with harsh black edges to keep us contained.

Mum screamed like that a long time ago. But I don't recall why. Brief flashes trickle into my conscious without context. Each attempt to recreate the memory causes the image to glitch and recede—a shroud swaddles my past, obscuring it.

The latest incarnation of Zenna is waiting for me on my easel, with a budding malice—self-assured and severe. So different to the peacefulness and refinement of the exhibition. In acrylic, she's sharp and definite. No longer a fantasy.

She's beside me, stroking my cheek. Her fingers burn into my skin, and I pull away.

Remember me.

I pull the duvet over my head, the pressure of her hand still firmly on my face. Nonsense, obviously. Impossible. The relentless murmuring rises until the voice is shouting, resonating around my head and obliterating my own thoughts.

Remember me!

"I don't want to."

You don't have a choice—you always do, in the end.

"You're just a dream. You're not real."

You're wrong. I'm so much more.

"Leave me alone!"

She grows in front of me, filling the room, and laughs—booming, reverberating off the walls, shaking me, pulsating through me. With a single finger, she holds me down. And I'm underwater, struggling to breathe, straining away from her. I can't escape—in a moment, I'll take my final gulp of air, and the cold, brackish ocean will fill my lungs.

I surge from the water, back into the room. Flying toward the canvas, I gouge into the paint with ragged fingernails. I grope for a weapon. Scissors. I press the point against her throat watching the canvas bow to the pressure. Harder. A hole develops.

"Leave me alone!" My voice is deep and guttural, raging.

I drive the scissors all the way, right up to the handles, and drag the blades down, tearing into her flesh as though it's nothing but paper.

Nathan bursts in. He presses my arms tight against my body and coerces the scissors from my hand. They drop to the floor, or he throws them, and they bounce off the carpet.

"What the hell are you doing?"

"She was pushing me under. I couldn't breathe."

Already, the words don't make sense. I knew what I was doing, but now I'm not sure. A moment ago, I wasn't here—I was somewhere else entirely.

I twist my body to escape his grasp. He holds tighter, hauling me toward the bed. I writhe and wrestle against him, digging my feet into the carpet to gain traction, pushing my arms apart in the hope of breaking his grip. We fall together onto my bed, and he pins me down. I kick in fury, growl in frustration.

"I'm not letting you go until you calm down."

I scowl and snarl, hating him. My efforts are futile; my strength diminished. I can't keep up the fight and my limbs slacken. He releases his grip and lies on his back beside me. My wrath subsides and I'm exhausted. My head is heavy; the dream evaporates.

"What was that all about?"

I don't reply because I don't know. Nothing makes sense. My dreams are memories, my thoughts are dreams. Reality is tentative. People are appearing and disappearing; voices are disjointed. Water rushes all around me. I'm submerged and drowning.

Oh, Jo-Jo, you're so close. Just a little longer.

I sit up with a start. "Did you hear that?"

"Hear what?"

NINE

B right sunshine peeks through the gap in the curtains. The road is busy with traffic but without the shrieks of kids on their way to school. It must be mid-morning, at least. I should be at work. I stumble out of bed and I'm immediately overcome by yesterday's vertigo. The floor's in motion—there's an underlying vibration, as though I'm on a train rather than solid ground, succumbing to the gentle rocking of the carriages.

Nathan's in the kitchen, clattering mugs and plates. I slide myself along the wall, toward the smell of bacon sizzling on the grill.

"Go back to bed," he says without turning, clipped and monotone. He's either annoyed or tired. "I've called the café for you. I'll bring your breakfast in."

"We don't have the staff to cover my shift. I'll call them back. They'll need me in."

"Your boss wasn't expecting you. He said he sent you home early yesterday?" He glances at me, expecting a reply, and I nod. "Then go back to bed."

I hesitate. "Is something wrong?"

He stirs the egg in the pan vigorously. "It's almost ready."

Nathan follows with our breakfasts. He drags a chair across to sit beside me. He starts to eat immediately. I push fluffy scrambled egg around the plate.

"I had a nightmare—it's not a big deal," I say when his scrutiny is overbearing.

"You were sleepwalking. You had scissors in your hand, you could have hurt yourself."

"Not me. Zenna was—"

"Zenna?"

It's absurd—I know it is. The dream has fragmented. There was something compelling me to fight. But it's lost now, and the more I try, the less there is to find.

"I've got a virus or something, a fever. You get weird dreams with a fever, don't you?" I shrug. Yes, yes you do, I confirm to myself. "I'll take some paracetamol, and I'll be fine in a couple of days."

Remember me, Jo-Jo.

"Jo. I—" He loads his fork with egg and smears brown sauce over the top.

"Has this happened before?" I ask cautiously. I don't want to know. "The nightmares and stuff? Is it something to do with my amnesia? Am I going crazy?"

"No." He leans forward and takes my hand, earnest and sincere. My fingers are icy compared to his. "No, you're not crazy."

But he ignores the other questions.

All the answers are here—in the crevices and shadows of my brain. Perhaps I should give up the search. Yet Zenna remains, taunting me. Her eyes burrow into me, her smirk troubles me. Lurking in my closed-door memory, concealed in my past.

"You can talk to me, you know. You don't have to lash out at defenseless paintings."

"But you're not telling me the truth."

Our fingers are still laced together, his thumb stroking my wrist as though it's completely natural. I savor the tingle it creates. His touch is soft and familiar; the stirrings of a memory loiter, unrealized.

I pull away abruptly, flustered.

He withdraws more slowly, scratching his fingers across the duvet reluctantly. "I guess I should ... I'm working here today, so just shout if you need me."

My gaze is firmly on my plate, trying to control my erratic breathing. "I will."

He closes the door behind him, and I inhale quickly and cough.

No, no, no. That shouldn't have ... What the hell? It's Nathan ... Nathe. We don't do *that*. Friends. Flatmates. It's all we are, all we want. We don't need anything else, we're happy.

People sometimes question our relationship, and we're always quick to point out *it's not like that*. But perhaps he wants it to be. Perhaps *I'm* quick to deny it, and he stays quiet.

I pick at the congealing egg, and then discard the plate on the floor. The pillow is rock-hard when my head hits it; the room sways as though I'm on a swing, gently pushing myself back and forth. I'm consoled into somnolence by the thump-thump of Nathan's computer keyboard. I don't ever want him not to be in the room next door, but one day it'll happen, won't it? One day, he'll find someone to love and he'll move on with his life. And I'll be here, anchorless.

When Zenna appeared beneath my paintbrush, months ago, she wasn't fully formed.

Only, I can't think of it as *months* anymore, can I? She's been leaching into my work for years.

So, when she appeared *this* time, before the portraits and discernible faces which I'd considered her origin, she wasn't fully *re*-formed. How could I have forgotten? I'd been painting a crowd scene, drenching my elongated Lowry-esque figures with rainbow tints. Bright and abstract.

From the left of the picture, a dark apparition loomed toward them. I checked my palette, convinced I hadn't even opened the black tube. And there it was, beside all the other colors.

"Where did you come from, eh?" I muttered, dabbing the wet paint. I wiped the black smudge on the tip of my finger across my painting shirt.

This presence, like a ghost sneaking in, dominated the picture; sinister and hostile in place of the fresh and lively scene I'd intended. With the Cerulean Blue, I attempted to paint over it, dappling the brush over the canvas to erase her, smearing long, dense lines. The shape was veiled but not hidden. As the paint dried, the shadowy figure re-emerged.

I crane my neck to hunt for her, in tattered pieces on the floor, where I left her, but she's gone. Nathan must have tidied up after he settled me back down last night. The scissors aren't here, either. A few chips of red paint on the carpet are the only signs of anything amiss.

In the corner of the room, my old sketchpads are piled on top of each other. I don't throw them away or store them in boxes; they remain in sight, my memoirs in pencil or pastel. My attempt to connect with who I was before. A diary, I suppose, in picture form.

I don't often open them, scared of what I might find. There must be a good reason for my brain to block out my memories—an event too shocking to bear, or an accident I'll never fully recover from. It's bravado when I tell myself I need to know—I have a habit of running away when the opportunity presents itself. The sketchpads are in full sight, but I never touch them.

What if they are the key, and I've been ignoring them all this time? What if, in them, my secrets are revealed?

I crawl over and wipe the woven layer of dust from the cover of the top book, lifting it to breathe in the warm, musty odor of old paper. The pages are crisp and yellow; when I flick through them, they produce a mellifluous sound. The book contains doodles of diners in coffee shops, buskers on street corners, shoppers and commuters, the joy on people's faces during a carnival, the despondency of an old man waiting for a bus. For some reason, dogs were a fascination for a while—their noses, paws, ears all being worked on and perfected.

There are likenesses of myself and my mother—or the vague concept I had of her at the time. She changes quite remarkably across the pages. I can't be sure if it's really her, if they were drawn before or after whatever calamity overcame me.

And Zenna, interwoven among us until it's hard to distinguish who's who. My fingers run over the sketches, following the indentations and bumps of Zenna's face. Subsequent books are packed full of her, unchanging. Page after page after page.

My eyes glaze over, my vertigo and nausea return. I lie down and Zenna's face is etched on the inside of my eyelids; her voice is strong and insistent.

Remember me!

I wish I could.

TEN

The sun sets and rises. Nathan works from home again. He cooks and sits beside me to eat—he says I need proper food, not the stuff I normally concoct for myself. He regards me with an unfathomable expression, as if about to say something, then smiles briefly and makes inane comments about the weather.

On Tuesday or Wednesday—I'm losing track of the days, they slither so easily into each other—Spencer texts to tell me my interview has been published, and Nathan rushes out to buy the paper. I'd forgotten all about it; I'm not sure I want to read it. But he flicks through and finds the right page, presenting it with a flourish. I'm confronted by a palm-sized photo of me beside *Zenna in the Sea,* and a headline which reads: Personal and Raw, Inscrutable Imagery.

I cover the photo with my hand. "Oh God, it's awful."

"No, it's lovely." Nathan sits on the edge of the bed and moves my hand from the page so he can read while I'm still cringing.

Spencer makes me sound fun and enchanting, graciously focusing on the exhibition rather than my memory loss. He reviews the paintings—he'd taken more notice than I assumed—and spends a couple of paragraphs reminiscing on the young adult he knew, which sounds vaguely like an obituary.

Nathan jabs his finger at the page. "He was at uni with us?"

"Yes. He said we were together for a bit. Do you know anything about that? I was at a disadvantage."

"Mmm, maybe. Before I knew you properly, perhaps. I don't remember him." He bristles slightly and continues to read with a pout. "Still, it's a good write-up. Well done." He kisses the top of my head.

Further down the page, Spencer writes, "The collection is raw and personal, an insight into a trauma either real or conceived by the artist."

Despite being submerged, Zenna is calm and composed in the title painting; very much untraumatized. Her smile is measured, her expression aloof. No one studying her would spot trauma of any kind—they'd see beauty and bewitch-ment, and be as overwhelmed by her as I am. Even in print, she beckons me, enticing me toward her.

Nathan removes the newspaper and folds it. "That's enough for today—I don't want you to get big-headed. If you're good, I'll let you read it again tomorrow. Or cut it out and frame it," he adds with a wink.

It takes a second to bring myself back. I smile. "Yeah, maybe."

***

As my dizziness retreats, I make it as far as the sofa. Nathan makes a nest with my duvet, and I snuggle into it while he cooks. Occasionally he calls through or pops his head around the door. I doze, letting these homely sounds filter through, jolting myself awake before any dream can take hold.

The voice is a wave of water, or a crowd all murmuring together. Nathan disappears; the flat splits wide open until I'm floating in a bubble high above London. The sound increases, and I cover my ears to block it out. I squeeze my eyes shut, scrunching my face, and when I open them, I'm in my duvet on the sofa and Nathan's dishing up in the kitchen.

We eat dinner on our laps, with a bottle of wine.

"So, you're all set for going back to work? Another day or two, just to make sure?"

"Actually, you know I mentioned visiting Mum? I was thinking I'd take a few days' leave and go now." I haven't been thinking anything of the sort. I try to bite back my words, even as they're spilling from my mouth.

"Are you up to the journey?"

"I'm fine." It's a faint vibration, hardly noticeable—just the whisper, the persistent voice in my ear.

His mouth twitches, but he says nothing.

"I just need to get away for a bit." I have to justify it, make it seem planned yet casual. Although why do I? Why do I need to explain myself to my flatmate, my friend? I wouldn't have this conversation with Lily. I'd say *I'm going to see my mum for a few days*, and she'd wish me a good trip.

"You don't need to go *there* to get away. Surely," he adds after a beat.

I sip wine and savor the taste for a second. "You don't think it's a good idea?"

"It's … out of the blue. You don't mention your mum much, and suddenly you want to spend all this time with her."

"It's not *all this time*. It's a day or two." Forkful of lasagna, sip of wine. "I'm starting to wonder if my nightmares are linked to home."

"I thought you'd only had a couple."

I shrug. "Mum's in them, that's why it's important I go. And you're in them. And … so's Zenna."

"Oh."

"It sounds stupid, doesn't it?"

He smirks. "Yes."

"It's like she's stalking me, or worse—haunting me." I let out a short hollow laugh. "Do you believe in ghosts?"

"No."

From the corner of the room, eyes watch me and my skin crawls.

"No, me neither." I push the remainder of my dinner around the plate and crunch into a fragment of crispy burned cheese. "A few days in Cornwall, fresh sea air, a proper pasty … I'll be back to normal in no time."

"You sound like you're trying to convince yourself."

"I don't know why you're making such a big deal about this."

"Because you want answers and there might not be any."

"There's a reason I lost my memory. I might find out what it is."

"What if the memories aren't all good ones? You might be trying to protect yourself from something bad."

I shake my head vehemently. "It wouldn't matter. You don't understand what it's like to live with chunks of yourself missing. Even if it *is* bad"—I take a deep breath because the realization is unexpected—"I need to know. Everything we are comes from the things we experience. Without them, I'm a blank page."

I think of my sketchbooks on the floor in my bedroom, dated for every single one of the last fifteen years. So much in them I don't recognize. I drain my glass and top it up, pouring until the liquid clings to the rim.

"There's a reason I don't have friends or relationships—I can't. Because I'm not a whole person. I'm not complete." I don't mean to cry, but tears run down my cheeks.

"You have me," he says softly.

"I know, but …" I exhale, reconsidering everything I was so sure of a minute ago.

"Perhaps we should check out some local support groups. There must be an Amnesiacs Anonymous somewhere?"

"I don't want a support group. I want to go home."

"I don't want you to get hurt."

"I won't get hurt."

He considers me carefully, considers his words. "You don't know what you'll discover."

"You're talking like *you* do."

"Fine." He gets up and snatches my plate from my lap. "It's nothing to do with me. If you want to go on this *quest* ..."

"Quest?" I scoff. "I'm not hunting dragons."

"You might as well be," he mutters, turning to the door.

"What the hell is that supposed to mean?"

He scowls. "Nothing. It means nothing." And without another word, he takes the plates to the kitchen and disappears into his room.

ELEVEN

I'm in front of a canvas far larger than anything I've attempted before. It stretches as high as a house, as wide as several double-decker buses end-to-end. Jumping to reach the top of it is pointless—I need a ladder. But suddenly, I don't, because I'm being lifted.

Zenna, again. She's blowing gently, and I'm gliding on the breeze she's creating. I hover like a kestrel, before recoiling in panic at the height I've achieved. She withdraws her breath and I plummet to the ground.

Her hand breaks free of the giant canvas; the paint cracks and flakes onto the floor. She's fascinated by her fingers branching into the real world. She wasn't expecting to be released from the confines of her acrylic prison—an arrogant smirk creeps across her face. She holds out her other arm and pushes her head through. Her shoulders follow. She slides from the painted version of herself as though being born.

There's a spotlight on us, casting eerie shadows across our faces. I hunt for the source, but, as with all nightmares, logic is diminished and there is none. My heart beats erratically, fearful of her, but without reason. She's mine—my creation, mine to control.

Her eyes flash with malice, so brief I discount it immediately. Just as quickly, she shrinks until she's only slightly taller than me. She folds me into her arms and strokes my hair. Such a tender maternal touch. I relax into her torso and rest my head against her chest. *I knew you'd find me.* Then she's gone.

I'm alone, bobbing on a stagnant ocean, stricken with foreboding.

The flat is dark and cold. My arm's gone dead, hanging off the edge of my bed. I try to cling to the dream, but it's already disintegrating. I extract myself from the duvet and rub my arm vigorously, enduring the agony of the blood returning.

Outside, the street is dormant. A lone cat skips from one shadow to the next; a taxi speeds past. Wind bristles through the magnolia tree in our front garden. My unease slowly subsides, but the image of Zenna remains with me. Her eyes ... there was something ruthless in them, something I've never painted nor envisaged.

Before the hug, I was ready to flee.

***

Half an hour later, I'm in the kitchen with a stuffed bag slung over my shoulder. I consider the melodrama of sneaking away overnight, then scribble a note for Nathan and prop it against the kettle.

The irregular hum of the North Circular hangs on the frosty air. My footsteps echo around the street, bouncing off the two-story houses. The light's on next door; the shadow of a baby being rocked in its parent's arms ripples on the curtains—newborn, brought home a few days ago.

I throw my bag into the boot of the car and slide into the driver's seat. Deep breath. Count slowly from ten to one— like Nathan taught me. Our windows are in darkness. I forgot to close the curtains so I can make out the line of the chimney breast and the edge of the TV. This is all wrong—I should wait until morning, talk to Nathan, to Lily. I should ask for other opinions.

Is this what I normally do, run away when life becomes difficult? Is it what I did before? Did I run away from my mother in Cornwall all those years ago?

The house disappears in the rear-view mirror. I turn left and head for the M4. The roads are busier than I'd expected—huge lorries delivering freight to supermarkets and cars transporting lone, weary workers to or from their nightshifts.

Clear of the city, the monotony of the motorway is soporific; the rhythm of the tarmac beneath my wheels is a lullaby. My eyes droop even though I've been on the road less than an hour. It was stupid to leave immediately—I should have waited until Nathan left for work. The hodgepodge of songs on Absolute Radio revives me until I can turn off at the next services.

The car park is spotted with vehicles spread out as if in the middle of a game of chess. Floodlights create stark shadows of the tree-lined boundary. The lack of people makes me skittish—my eyes flicker toward every piece of litter fluttering across the tarmac, every flash of headlight from the motorway.

I scurry across the car park and into the building, shielding my eyes against the painful fluorescence. But with the welcoming staff behind the counter awaiting my order, I exhale my relief. My hands, balled into tight fists, begin to relax.

At half-past two, there's only a skeleton service available. The smell of coffee and bacon pervades the café; my stomach rumbles. I haven't eaten since Nathan's lasagna hours ago. The cakes on display are gooey and appealing, but I'm not sure if it's breakfast or midnight snack time.

I order a chocolate muffin and cappuccino and take the tray to a table beside the window. Lights shine onto the glass, so it becomes a mirror—a hollow-eyed, dazed woman eating cake stares back at me.

This is irrational, pointless even. I have no idea what I'll say when I see Mum. If I drove back the way I've just come, I'd be home before dawn. I could throw away the note I left for Nathan and go to bed, and he'd never realize I was gone.

Yet, I remain where I am and sip the coffee, avoiding my disapproving reflection. I pick at the muffin, munching the tiny chunks of chocolate and letting them melt in my mouth. The chocolate soothes me.

You don't know what you'll discover. That's what Nathan said. *What if the memories aren't all good?* He said that too, without explanation, keeping secrets.

I rest my shoulder against the window and tilt my head to the cold glass. It's still pitch-black; the sun won't rise for hours. It'll take four to get to Cornwall—too early to knock on someone's door and yell, "Surprise!"

My body slackens. My fatigue is so acute it doesn't matter where I am, I just want to sleep. At a rough guess, I'm approaching twenty-one hours without proper sleep. Just a moment's snooze and I'll be ready to drive again. My limbs sag; my mouth gapes open. The ebb and flow of the voices in my head serenade me.

The eerie sound of wind rattling windows and doors and the uncomfortable molded plastic chair make it impossible to drift off for more than a few minutes before I shudder myself awake. I take my sketchpad from my bag instead. I glimpse my worried, ashen reflection, and draw myself. The concentration makes me appear severe and morose; the shading turns me into a ghost.

On the opposite page, I draw my mother. I have her lean across the table, as though she's sharing gossip about the neighbors with me. I give her a keen, mischievous smile and raise her eyebrows in glee. This never occurred—I left home long before we could sit together as adults, as equals. Our previous, mislaid relationship will be replaced by a brand new version.

When I examine what I've drawn, I recall the softness of the towel when she dried me after a bath, the chemical taste of lipstick when she tucked me into bed, the gleam of her freshly washed hair when she drove me to school. I close the pad because I don't want to think about her anymore.

The caffeine and sugar kicks in, and I'm alert and raring to go. I gobble the rest of the muffin, pack up my bag, and buy a flat white to take with me.

Outside, an icy drizzle threatens to become heavier. I'm struck by the romance of the rain falling in the beam of the floodlights, floating like snow.

And I'm driving again.

The cat's eyes lighting my path, the road unvaried beneath my wheels. The silhouettes of high banks and trees following me ominously. Like ghosts. A child laughs.

And I'm driving, and driving, and …

Traffic increases as I reach the outskirts of Bristol—early commuters on the move. Road signs count down the miles. Closer and closer. No turning back. By six, I'm at Exeter. Hungry and weary, I stop for breakfast, and it's a relief to stretch my legs and breathe in the fresh yet fume-filled air. I line up with an increasing number of travelers—young couples on weekend breaks, parents and young kids, friends heading out for early shopping bargains. I belong among these people; I'm no longer an anomaly.

It'll take another ninety minutes to reach Mum's house, my childhood home. Soon, I'll be on the A38, a hilly snaking road; no more motorway. Soon, I'll open the windows and let the wind blow through my hair. Soon, I'll be in front of the house, my hand held up to press the doorbell.

Soon.

TWELVE

These are some of the things I *do* remember, butted together like a badly ordered photo album.

Sitting alone in a pub on my twenty-third birthday. I must have gone with someone, but I don't remember who. There was a band, and someone—a nameless, faceless creature—asked them to play "Free Falling" because it was my favorite song at the time. They were good, but by ten-thirty the pub was practically deserted, and I was sitting alone in the corner. Whoever I was with had vanished. Or perhaps it's just where my memory falters.

Enduring a long, cramped, sweaty bus trip to Liverpool. I sat beside an old lady who kept nudging me with her elbows as she knitted and smelled of Werther's Originals. The sluggish motion and stuffy air made me nauseated for most of the journey. I have no idea what reason I had for traveling north. But I definitely hate traveling by coach.

Standing on a bridge, staring down into a black, slow moving river. I was shaking. I was going to jump. Something terrible had happened. And then something—someone, perhaps—stopped me. The moment passed, I have bristling resentment when I think of it, although I'm happy I survived. At the time, my recovery was slow.

Then there are the smaller things—snippets of conversation during a funeral, dancing to Radiohead at a festival, fidgeting in the dark waiting for a surprise party to begin. My life dribbles into my subconscious and drifts away, like scenes from a film I watched years ago.

When I walk past a bakery, the smell of fresh bread evokes the joy of spending time with my grandmother, but not her appearance. Fresh cut grass makes the soles of my feet tingle as though I'm walking barefoot upon it. The growl of a hurtling motorbike makes my heart beat in my throat. I grasp these moments, longing for the narrative to expand.

I lived on someone's sofa and woke each morning with a crick in my neck. I worked in Starbucks and Costa and several independent coffee shops—I've kept the name tags.

I was engaged.

Buried in a box, tucked away beneath my bed, I have the ring. I can't give it away, but I pretend it's not there. I hope I'll wake one day and recall who gave it to me—someone lost to me, or I to him. Recently, I've wondered if it was Spencer, but we'd have been far too young to be thinking of marriage. Any relationship with him would have been fun and flighty, I imagine.

I met Lily.

I met Nathan.

In my head, they're paired. Lily-and-Nathan. But that's not right. They're not friends with each other, the way I am with them—they're acquaintances. We go for drinks together, but they don't phone each other for a chat or meet up without me.

At some low point in my life, Nathan offered me his spare room.

I remember him asking about my family once, about my childhood, why I left Cornwall. I said I didn't know, and he studied me with sadness and pity, as though my life was somehow worse for not knowing. As if I was lacking the fundamentals. We've argued about it since, when my frustrations have overwhelmed me and driven me to hysteria.

I know I miss living by the sea, even though the daily details evade me. I dream of waves crashing against rocks on stormy days, of balmy evenings lying in the garden with friends, of seagulls screeching me awake in the mornings. Yet the idea of swimming in the sea terrifies me, and pool swimming is just as daunting.

I know I'm not who I'm supposed to be. How can I be, with so much of myself nestled so deeply within?

***

Past Plymouth and across the Tamar, the dual carriageway converts into a road with three lanes randomly changing priority, and finally filtering down to just two. This is the joy and horror of driving in Cornwall. Roads squeeze through small stone-cottage hamlets and follow the hills and valleys once traversed by farmers and traders. There are no straight roads here, no Roman legacy.

This knowledge is deep-seated, as though I regularly drive this route—an infused awareness.

It's light, albeit with high, impenetrable clouds. I'm captivated by the space and scale of the countryside—the density of London far behind me. I stretch to catch the splendor of yellow and purple crops on the hillsides and the clumps of villages with spires sprouting into the sky.

The road narrows, sweeping and curling around the woodland-wrapped hill, slicing into it as the slope falls away on the left and banks steeply on the right. When I meet vans and large 4x4s coming the other way, I pull toward the drop to allow them to pass. Parts of the road, eroded after severe storms, crumble and I inch my wheels as close as I dare.

Around the final corner into the village, I gasp as I absorb the sheer magnificence. It's a flat oasis surrounded by steep hills flecked with houses. A river, parallel to the road I've just driven, flows toward the beach. The sea is calm, steel gray, mirroring the sky. Where the sun breaks through, out toward the horizon, the light shimmers and skips on the waves. It's just before eight o'clock; the beach is dusted with pre-work dog-walkers and a paddleboarder is exiting the water.

My mother's house clings to the far side of the valley. Just another couple of turns and I'll be there. My stomach is hollow, groaning with hunger and nerves equally. I can't do it. I can't go up there. I can't knock on her door as though it's something I do every single day. What was I thinking? If I haven't been back in so long, will she even want to talk to me?

I park in one of the bays facing the sea and slouch in my seat, my adrenaline dissipating. Does Mum have a dog? Is she striding out along the sand with it? Will she pass me on her way home? My breathing escalates until I'm on the verge of hyperventilating. I take deep breaths, holding each one until my lungs ache, and exhale as slowly as possible. Ten, nine, eight …

A shadow passes over me, and through me, and I'm plunging into the water. It's cold and I shudder, scrambling to be pulled back out. It's momentary. I'm in the car again, disorientated and dizzy.

I glance at my watch. I've been here for over an hour. A couple of swimmers head back to their pile of clothes, some of the dog-walkers are sitting on the café terrace, a lone surfer paddles, waiting for a wave which probably won't come for a while. All the normal things. And me, out of place, no longer fitting in.

From this angle, Mum's house is screened by trees and other houses. I tap my fingers on the steering wheel. If I wanted, I could turn around and leave. She'd never know how close I was. Back in London, I could help to market my exhibition, and make a start on the next one. It makes sense to go back.

Yet, I'm still here.

A couple of minutes later, I'm parking in front of her garage. I glance at the scribbled address on the seat beside me, just to be certain. The house is high above the road. Steps rise beside the garage and a path continues through the garden to the 1970s terrace. It must have been an easy climb for an energetic seven-year-old. Now, my legs ache from the exertion, and from my fixed position of the past few hours.

I press the bell.

I have déjà vu. At different times of the day, under various weather conditions, and with different colored fingernails, I reach toward the door and press the bell. It's not possible; I haven't come home like this before.

I press again. Perhaps she's not in. Perhaps she moved. I've considered it in jest over the years—as a joke to shock people—but I didn't really expect she wouldn't be here anymore. I squint through the frosted glass to check for movement. A black shape looms into view.

Oh God. I rest my hand on the wall to prevent myself running away. Turning and fleeing would be so easy. My stomach churns. Hello. Just say hello. My heart beats frantically. This is a mistake, a stupid mistake. Is it too late to run?

The door opens, and Mum's right there in front of me.

I say nothing.

She flicks ash from her cigarette outside the door and exhales smoke into the air above me.

Hello. Just say hello.

I'm frozen, blank. As though I've woken from a vivid

dream into an alternative reality. I thought I'd cry and be filled with happiness, and she'd rush forward to hug me with relief and euphoria.

"Hello," I say at last, and my voice is tiny.

THIRTEEN

The hall is dark and long, and I'm immediately over-whelmed—not with being here, with something else, something bigger and unspecified. My body is dragging, as though someone is pulling on my arms, preventing me advancing further into the house. An icy chill encircles me.

My legs almost give way beneath me; the voice surges around me. I catch myself on the bannister and pause until the vertigo passes.

I'd assumed there'd be photos on the wall, all of us together—me at different ages, my parents' wedding photo, a birthday gathering in a pub—hooks for my memories to snag on. But the walls are bare. The chipped pale blue paint needs refreshing; there are scuff marks at shopping-bag level and dark shadows where frames used to hang. I run my finger along the marks.

Mum's already bustling around in the kitchen at the end of the hall. "Come through," she calls.

I don't have memories of living here. It's not comfortable or relaxing. Surely, in my mother's house—the house I grew up in—I'd drop my bag in the hall, offer to put the kettle on, grab her stash of dark chocolate Hobnobs. I'd actually know if she liked the dark chocolate ones. I'd call out in easy conversation from room to room or walk into the lounge and collapse onto the sofa to recover from the journey. Possibly, I expected all of it—to walk through the front door and have my life miraculously restored.

But, instead, I hesitate over whether to remove my shoes before I follow her.

To my left is the lounge, and straight ahead is the kitchen. Mum's gathering things from the dining table and shoving them into cupboards, making space for me. She slams the doors shut and leans against the counter.

I'm ungainly and gangly, crossing my arms then letting them dangle by my side as if I've forgotten how to stand. I'm overthinking it.

"Sit down," she says eventually, taking a seat at the table. "You look tired."

"I left early."

She's austere and reserved, wearing a shapeless brown skirt and fraying beige cardigan with woolly tights. Her hair is brushed back into a taut ponytail, and her hair and skin are both gray. She's weary and haggard—nothing like my drawings. Where's her radiance? Where's the color? She's older than I thought—sixty, maybe. If I'm thirty-three, that's about right, I guess.

We haven't hugged. It's a gaping omission, leaving me uncertain. I remain on my feet, waiting for something poignant to happen, waiting to be a daughter visiting her mother after so long apart rather than a guest making small talk at a party.

"Did you have a good journey?"

"Yeah, the roads were quiet." Pause. My turn. "How've you been? You're looking well."

"Thank you. I'm good."

The house has a disheveled appearance, nothing obviously new or revamped to comment on. I smile ambiguously. When is it a good time to tell the woman who gave birth to you that you have no recollection of your life together and to all intents and purposes, she's a stranger? She's not someone I can confide in—she's not Nathan or Lily. Spencer was the last person I explained myself to, and he left me no choice because he asked outright.

"So ... where's Dad?" I glance to the door, expecting him to appear from upstairs and call me *Sprout* or some other childhood nickname.

"Durham," she says as easily as replying *in the garden* or *just popped to the shop*. "Where he lives now."

My cheeks burn. Shit. I've given everything away. She'll detect my deception and throw me out of the house. I slide into the chair, in defeat, awaiting her questions.

"He only moved recently. He was in Aberdeen before then, of course. He tells me where he is in case we need him—one day, I'd love to tell him we don't."

"Oh." My face flushed with duplicity, I take slow breaths to calm myself.

His absence in my memory has always bothered me less than anything else, and perhaps that's why—because he left a long time ago. A face would be nice, a small memento—at one time, he would have been the most important man in my life. But it's not him I draw, trying to pin his likeness into my consciousness. It's not him who brought me here.

"Tea!" Mum claps her hands and stands abruptly so the table wobbles. A statement rather than a question. "I expect you could do with a cuppa." Another statement.

"Only if you're making one."

"I'm *always* making one. Unless you prefer coffee? I can ..." She frowns, her hand resting on the kettle's switch.

"No, tea's great. Thank you."

"How long are you staying?"

"I don't know. I haven't thought about it. I just wanted to see you." Needed to, I *needed* to see you.

"Well." She stretches her arms out to the side, presenting herself. "Here I am."

Yes, here she is. Here *we* are.

Her arms are assuming the position of inviting a hug—but I can't. I'm rooted to the chair. I *should* want to—I think I do—but the wall between us is unfathomable and complicated, blocking our path.

The kettle boils, breaking the deadlock. Mum sets her mug on the counter and hunts for another, opening a couple of overhead cupboards before finding one, as if she doesn't use a second mug often, as if she has no need to.

I picture her alone, month after month, pacing the house—waiting for something new to happen, for someone to knock on the door like I did today. I imagine the TV switched on just for the noise and companionship—from the morning breakfast programs all the way to the regional news at half-past ten, hitting each makeover and quiz and cookery show in between.

Alone. And it's my fault. Perhaps she *was* once the vivacious character of my sketches; perhaps the grief of me leaving drove it out of her.

We take our drinks into the cluttered lounge. There are too many side tables in here. Too many cushions on the sofa. There are books stacked in front of rammed shelves and framed IKEA prints hanging on the walls. One painting—on the far wall, almost tucked behind a bookcase—is a watercolor of the beach, taking the viewer along the coastline further down into Cornwall. It's a similar style to some of mine, a few little flourishes here and there. But I didn't paint this one, I don't think. I move closer, to get a better look. In the bottom left corner, a figure is almost visible—faded, as though someone's tried to erase it.

"Oh, that old thing ..." Mum says dismissively. "Come and sit down."

There doesn't seem to be space for me. I wander to the large window, to the simplicity of the vast ocean. As Mum clears a spot, she makes idle conversation, but she's so far away. I'm bobbing on the waves again, succumbing to the ebb and flow. Seawater surges toward me. Someone calls out.

I turn into the room and the sensation ceases. Another daydream. It's been almost twenty-eight hours since I slept—dreams are seeping into reality because there's nothing to prevent them.

"If I lived here," I say, cutting into Mum's disjointed sentences, "I'd sit at this window all day."

"Sometimes I do." But she's already nestled among the cushions on the sofa, so today is obviously not one of those times.

My misgiving at being here is increasing. Nathan will have woken and found my note. He may have sworn in fury and thrown it across the room. My face flashes with shame—he was right, this was a bad idea. All I needed to do was go out and get drunk with Lily or lie on the grass in Hyde Park and stare at the sky. I have no reason to be here. I should have stayed home and painted, committing my confusion to canvas until there was nothing left in my head.

I examine the room for something I recognize, something to attach me to this life. There must be something to hint at my childhood—a misshapen pottery bowl or a favorite book on one of these shelves. Otherwise, this is just another house, just another lounge. It's not home.

"Are you still in London? What are you doing now?"

"Yes. I'm a barista."

"Is that a *proper* job for someone your age?"

I bite my lip. "I enjoy it."

"And you're still painting."

"Uh, yeah. How did …?"

"Your exhibition is in the paper." She waves her hand toward the pile of newspapers on the coffee table. "You said you were a barista."

Zenna in the Sea is a thumbnail on the header of the *Independent*, advertising the article within. As small as she is, I feel a pull toward her, the voice becoming urgent and clamorous before settling to a gentle hum when I turn the paper over.

"Painting's just a hobby."

"Some hobby! Exhibitions, superb reviews across the board, interviews. That's a career, Jo, not a hobby."

I shrug. "I guess." *How would you know? How would you know anything about me?*

We resort to silence which quickly becomes intolerable. I have a hundred things I want to say, but no idea how to begin. The rigid expression on Mum's face suggests the same of her. If we're this uncomfortable in each other's presence now, it'll only get worse the longer I stay.

"I'm sorry I turned up like this. I think it was a mistake. Perhaps it's best if I leave."

She considers me, almost as though she'd forgotten I was in the room. "You should at least stay for lunch. You're exhausted." She jumps up, hindering my path to the front door, unnervingly close. "Or you could stay the night, if you want. I can make up the bed in the spare ... in *your* room." She motions toward the room above us—which is probably hers, given the layout of the house—but I nonsensically glance at the 70s Artex ceiling.

I relent, relax, feel the pressure of fatigue pressing against my forehead. "That would be nice," I force myself to say, because maybe it will be.

FOURTEEN

I sit on the bed in my old room, with its magnolia walls and patterned pink curtains, and I'm convinced I never had it decorated like this. There are no childhood remnants or teenage memorabilia. No wardrobe either, just a chest of drawers, a flowery tub chair, and a bedspread instead of a duvet. The air has the faint odor of mothballs.

This room is at the rear of the house, backing onto a steep garden and, beyond it, the hill curves around to enfold the village. I have a brief insight of running up it, hand-in-hand with someone whose face I can't see. I'm laughing and dancing, and yet I have no idea who I'm clinging to. The moment I try to snatch a glimpse, to quickly peek sideways and outsmart myself, the vision weakens.

With relief, I sink into the mattress, submitting to my lassitude. The tension in my body defuses. Bright colors flutter around me. I endeavor to catch them, but they pour through my fingers like ribbon.

Mum coughs from the door to attract my attention. I open my eyes and blink against the stark daylight. She doesn't come into the room but leans against the jamb. "Okay?"

"Yes, thank you. I just closed my eyes for a moment."

"You were asleep."

I yawn, groggy with a blunt headache. "Just for a moment," I repeat.

"It's half-past eleven."

I clamber off the bed. "Sorry, I didn't realize." And, once more, we're clumsy with each other.

"You were blowing bubbles like you used to when you were a baby," she says wistfully. "I'm sorry about earlier. I wasn't sure what to say. It's been a long time."

"I should have called."

"No, it's fine," she says, almost overlapping me. She lingers, sliding her forefinger across the top of the chest of drawers and checking for dust, smoothing the corner of the bedspread. "Do you fancy a walk? Clear your head?"

"Sure."

Mum peels herself away from the door. I grab my coat and bobble hat and follow. She's changed her clothes. She's wearing scruffy biker boots and jeans now. Again, her age eludes me. She's about forty, fresh-faced and enthusiastic.

Conversation is sporadic and short-lived. I dig my hands into my coat pockets and hunch my shoulders against the biting sea breeze. Mum repeatedly glances across at me. When we reach the beach, she pauses, querying if I want to continue.

I nod but freeze before my foot touches the soft sand. I'm dizzy again; the air is thick and hard to inhale. The sea, far out, is churning and menacing—Midnight Green, if I were to paint it. Clouds scamper past, darkening as they move in from the Channel. There's no fixed point; the sea and clouds and horizon all move independently. I hold my hands to the side of my head, trying to keep myself still.

"Jo?"

Mum touches my shoulder and I jump. I'd forgotten she was there.

"Sorry. What?"

"I'd like you to meet a friend of mine, Rose." She moves to reveal a cheerful white-haired lady with a generous smile. "Rose, this is my daughter Jo, she's just arrived from London."

Rose steps forward and takes both my hands and squeezes. "Jo, it's so lovely to meet you at last." A shadow of uneasiness crosses her face—sympathy and kindness are thrown into the mix. Her eyes flicker to Mum continually. "Your mum's told me so much ... I saw your article in the paper, too. Congratulations."

"Hello. Nice to meet you. Thank you."

They both expect me to say more, but what else is there? After a moment, they resume their conversation and I wander away like a bored child.

Once again, I'm on the threshold of the beach, one foot hovering indecisively above the sand.

One step ...

And another.

Both feet on the beach, I'm unaccountably anxious. Another, and another. Moving further away from the road where Mum and Rose are still talking.

"Not too far, Jo-Jo," she calls from my past. Because I was the child who loved to run off and hide, who giggled with glee while my parents were frantic.

A memory! Not a fleeting image or vague perception. A fully formed picture, solid and palpable. And it's gone. My head is empty for a moment, then slowly fills with the enticing sound of surging waves and the sight of the vivid ocean again.

I advance tentatively across the fine sand at the top of the beach, my feet sinking into it. Further along, I slip and slide over rounded shingle and large pebbles which crunch together beneath my boots. I'm drawn to the water, even though something terrible will happen ... has happened ... is happening.

Dreams and fragmented moments and reality all clash

together, bouncing off each other. I can't distinguish what's genuine and what's imagined. The beach spins around, or I spin it. Together, we're in motion. Unsettled and unbalanced, I stumble on seaweed and topple with my feet tangled.

Remember. Remember me.

My heart races. I struggle to catch my breath. I don't have my bearings. I'm lost, alone. Everything is alien. Mum's beside me in an instant, and I cling to her.

"It's okay, Jo. I'm here. Are you all right? Are you hurt?" She helps me to my feet and brushes damp sand from my coat. "This was a bad idea. We should have stayed home."

"I'm fine," I say absently. My ankle is swelling within my boot, throbbing. When I put my weight on it, I flinch and hobble.

"Come on, why don't we go to the pub and get some lunch?"

The Smugglers is a sprawling building on the outside, but warm and cozy with beamed ceilings once we step through the door. Wood and brick throughout make it homely. Small tables are placed sparsely, so the bar area is spacious and laid-back.

The hubbub of chatter, of clattering cutlery and clinking glasses, circulates. Waiting staff dart from the kitchen to the tables, removing dinner plates and bringing desserts. Mum guides me to one of the tables close to the bar.

"Hi, Craig," Mum calls brightly, hanging her coat over the back of a chair. "This is my daughter, Jo—I told you about her, the artist."

He looks up briefly from the pint he's pouring, and nods. "Nice to meet you, Jo. What can I get you both today?"

She tells people about me. I regard her with interest. Rose, this barman—how many others? It's a strange contradiction to our relationship, and I'm unsure how to react. I settle into my chair and observe Mum's interaction with the people she greets by name. She's spritely and unaged.

Standing at the bar, she asks what I'd like to drink and relays it to the barman as though he hasn't heard. She grabs two menus from the rack and wanders back. In all my theories and visualizations, she never resembled the person in front of me.

"Are you here for long?" he calls across.

I shrug. "A couple of days?"

I avoid looking at Mum—we haven't discussed my plans, so she'll be listening keenly. I flick through the menu while they continue to chat. She crosses her legs and swings her foot around. Craig brings our drinks across and remains beside us while we decide on our meals.

"How's your ankle?" Mum asks, once we're alone again.

I make circles under the table with my foot, wincing as part of the movement sends pain along my leg. "Sore."

"What happened?"

I try to recall how I became oddly disorientated. My head must have still been groggy from my nap. "I just fell."

I lean back and chug my cider, absorbing the laughter and cheerfulness of the groups and couples. They chat effortlessly; none of them are strained or nervous.

"This is a nice place," I say, when our silence becomes too loud and obtrusive.

"Yes. I come here quite a lot. I'm on the darts team."

"Oh. That's nice."

Our meals arrive and we delve in. We both ordered the carbonara—I turn the spaghetti on my fork until it slides off and start again.

"Do you work?" I ask, blurting out the first thing which comes to mind, regretting such a stupid question immediately.

"I do book-keeping for a couple of local businesses. I was made redundant a while back. It's a nice way to slide into retirement, and it keeps me busy."

"I didn't know you were made redundant."

She hesitates. "Why would you?"

It's not a malicious comment; it's matter of fact. And she's right—there's no reason for me to have. Even so, it seems remiss. Although, no more so than Mum not knowing I work in a coffee shop.

"Do you spend much time on the beach?"

Her eyes flicker to the door, to the direction of the sea. We can't see it from here; the pub is set back and down a small incline. "Not so much. You get used to having it right on your doorstep—it's not a novelty anymore. It's like walking along a pavement."

"Oh no. It's beautiful. I could set up my easel and paint the sea all day."

"You could?" She studies me, with concern or intrigue, it's hard to decipher. She finishes her gin and tonic and considers the empty glass. "Another?"

We order raspberry cheesecake, both proclaiming it our favorite. In truth, any dessert is my favorite. I'm full, but I don't want to leave this lively pub to sit in Mum's claustrophobic lounge. It's late afternoon—the longer we remain here, the less time we'll be alone later.

No, no, no … This isn't how it should be. We ought to be able to find something to talk about. We should be able to sit companionably, and not have it be weird. But nothing about this is normal. We're working far too hard to act naturally.

Around us, diners are leaving, replaced by couples and families wrapped up in ski jackets and scarves—people who've walked the beach and, as the sun begins to set, are in need of a drink to warm themselves. The ease of these people contrasts with our embarrassment.

We eat our cheesecakes and nurse our empty glasses.

"Another drink?" I ask, but Mum shakes her head, which is probably a good thing. Today has been the longest day, and it's not even five o'clock.

FIFTEEN

D usk folds over the village—a burgundy hue lies down on top of us. From the houses on the opposite side of the valley, lights sparkle like stars.

I open the lounge window and let the sharp, fresh air rush in. I lean out to listen to waves lapping against the shore, but the wind is blowing in the wrong direction, pushing the sound away. The occasional car whizzes along the single road which runs through the village. For extended moments, I hear nothing at all—such a difference to the constant activity at home.

Home. Nathan! I should call him. But I'm not sure what I'd say. I don't understand enough about the situation to share it with anyone, not even Nathan. I could at least tell him I arrived safely.

I wave my mobile in the air and pace around the room.

"You won't get a signal. You'll have to use the landline." She points to the handset and puts a bottle of wine and two glasses on the table. "I thought this might be easier if we had a drink."

"I'll be back in a minute." I grab the phone, and Mum puts a glass in my hand. I take both up to my room. The phone doesn't ring for long. "Hi Nathe."

"Jo! I've been worried about you."

"I'm at Mum's."

"I saw the note."

"Are you mad at me?"

"No." I imagine him running his hand through his hair or creasing his forehead as he considers the correct, courteous response. "I'm not mad. I didn't mean to cause a fight, I'm sorry. How is it?"

I glance at the door I left ajar and lower my voice. "It's weird. We're hyper polite, and we have nothing to say to each other."

"What did you expect?"

"I don't know—that my whole life would come flooding back the moment I walked in the door? That all my questions would be answered, and my hallucinations would disappear."

"Hallucinations? You never said anything."

Stupid to mention it. "It's not important." Stupid to give him more reason to worry. "And it didn't happen anyway."

I lean on the windowsill, peering up at the top of the hill, just a silhouette against the final glimmer of daylight. I open one of the drawers, then another. At the back of the bottom one is an ancient, threadbare rabbit. One ear's half-torn, held on with a few strands of thread, the other is chew-stained. I hug it, waiting for the pang of childhood joy to overwhelm me. It doesn't. I drink wine instead.

"She hasn't mentioned the argument either—I expected her to say something, even if it was to demand an apology."

"What argument?"

"The one we had, the reason I left home. We haven't talked in years—there's got to be a reason." The decrepit rabbit is still in my arms; I stroke his ear. "Anyway, you were right. I shouldn't have come."

"I didn't want to be."

"I must love her. I must have our entire life together

locked away, up here." I tap the side of my head. "I ought to have that, at least." The rabbit, this room, my childhood—all hidden.

"How long are you staying?"

"A day, maybe two. Not long."

"Take it slowly, yeah." He pauses. "I have to go—you'll be okay?"

"I'll be fine. See you soon."

I throw the phone onto the bed. I smooth my hand across the bedspread, the way Mum did earlier, and pick at the woven edges.

"Jo, are you coming back down?"

"In a minute."

I tuck the rabbit under the blanket and rest his worn head on my pillow.

***

I remember ...

No, it's gone again—a momentary sensation, of holding someone, *hugging* someone.

Or a toy. The rabbit perhaps. Nestling it in the crook of my arm and taking it everywhere with me.

Jo-Jo, remember me ...

It's twilight; gray and dull, again. I yawn and try to sit up. The blanket is tight against my torso, trapping my arms by my side. Someone's sitting on the edge of the bed, and I'm rolling into them.

"Mum?"

The figure laughs sharply. "Of course not."

I can't make out a face. I blink a few times, re-focusing, cutting through the haze of the half-light. But she's still there, encroaching. She touches my cheek, but I don't feel anything.

Zenna?

***

I wake again, properly. My head is foggy, and I'm hungry and thirsty in equal measure. I stretch to the corners of the bed, and expect to smell frying bacon and have Nathan mustering me for breakfast before remembering where I am.

Rain pulses against the window. The curtains are open and dark, stagnant clouds hang in the sky. I'm weighed down—but not with sadness or regret or any meaningful emotion. Just the residual solidity of a dream.

My head pounds when I sit up. I recall all the wine I drank last night at Mum's insistence. It was a bad idea, but she kept refilling our glasses. There was laughter, not many service-able words after a certain point. It might have helped. Or we might have said some horrible things I haven't remembered yet.

I shuffle my pillows until I'm propped up slightly, trying to find a position where I'm not nauseated. Gradually, I'm lucid enough to consider a hunt for food and water. I tumble out of bed and fumble around the floor for my clothes.

Downstairs, Mum's bright and cheerful, giving the impression of being awake for several hours. Her hair's damp from the shower; there's a light covering of makeup on her face. Did she not drink as much as me? Did she pour more into my glass each time, or tip her excess into the rubber plant when I wasn't looking?

"Morning," she says when I hover uncertainly at the door.

The radio's blasting out something by Ed Sheeran, and pain sears through my temples. I shrink back from the fluorescent light. I slide onto a chair and rest my head on the table.

"Egg and toasted soldiers? You used to love them when you were little. I thought it would be fun to have them this morning."

"Uh … Thanks. Is there any coffee?"

She flicks the switch on the kettle, and it boils immediately. She pours the water, offers sugar—I shake my head and groan—and adds a splash of milk before setting the mug in front of me with a thud which resonates along the table.

"What time is it?"

"Ten-thirty."

"You should have woken me."

"I came in, but you were fast asleep, so I left you. It's not a problem." She turns the egg timer as the water begins to boil. As the sand vanishes from the top chamber, she sweeps the pan off the hob.

Two egg cups are already set out, and she slides the eggs into them. The toast pops—she butters and cuts them into narrow strips. All of it done in a blur of activity.

"I've got a meeting at twelve. Will you be all right by yourself for a couple of hours? I'll cancel if ..."

I smash off the tops of both eggs with my spoon so the yolk oozes. "I was going to go back today."

"Not in this state, Jo. You can barely keep your eyes open."

My stomach churns with the first mouthful of toast, and I acquiesce. I'm exhausted and drained, mentally fatigued by everything that's happened over the past thirty-six hours.

"I'll go for a walk or something, then. Or I might sit in the garden and draw."

"You can borrow some of my old paints, if you like."

"You used to paint? Oh, is that yours in the lounge—the beach one?"

"Uh, yeah."

"It's good."

She dismisses the compliment with a wave of her hand. "I've got some old canvases too. I'll pull them out for you when I get back."

She's gone before I have time to reply, dashing upstairs to grab her boots or her bag. When she returns, her face is a stranger's again, her deportment is altered. Suddenly, she's just another random person, an illusion I'll reproduce in acrylic.

SIXTEEN

To clear my hangover, I take a shower. But I can't relax. Unknown sounds startle me, and I imagine people breaking into the house to rifle through my things. Or attack me with a large carving knife.

Once the water stops, the lack of noise is even more disturbing. My reflection slowly emerges through the steam. It swims, and—just like Mum earlier—transforms into a stranger in front of me. I'm depleted and gaunt, vaguely resembling Zenna.

On the landing, I peer into Mum's bedroom—an invisible barricade prevents me going any further. As a child, I would only go in when she was there—jumping into her bed on Sunday mornings before she was properly woken or to help her dress for a night out before the babysitter arrived. It was a privilege.

A variety of boxes are stacked on top of each other and clothes burst from the wardrobe and drawers. A pile of books has toppled over and spread across the carpet. Unpaired shoes tumble from under the bed.

I amble around the house, trying to fix on something I recall—the pictures on the walls, the selection of sheep ornaments on the mantelpiece, the yellowing Paignton Zoo snow globe. None of it elicits attachment.

In the kitchen, I make coffee. I open cupboards and consider the single plate, mug, and bowl within easy reach on the lower shelf, while the rest of the set is higher. There are pretty glass dessert bowls and ramekins covered with dust in another cupboard. An unopened pasta maker, cookie cutters in various shapes and sizes, several platters as though she spends her weekends throwing lavish dinner parties. Which I doubt.

Is this her life? Is this what I've done to her?

The house is airless, so I sit in the front garden with my mug and sketchpad. The feeble heat of the sun warms my face; the mug heats my hands. The wind off the sea wafts through my hair. The constant voices in my head have retreated—only a vague ripple remains, the concentric circles of a small stone dropped in a pond.

Zenna, however, is stronger. No longer the enigmatic muse for my collection or the siren tempting me away. She's unsettling and ominous, slinking from my dreams to stand beside me. In twilight, I catch a fleeting glimpse of her. I close my eyes and I am alone.

I sketch a window—shading the rain-splattered glass and the reflection of autumnal trees, with rough, jagged branches pointing into the sky like witches' fingers. With Deep Cadmium, I hint at sunlight glinting off the panes.

Every time the curve of an eye or suggestion of a mouth materializes, I smudge the pastel and start again. I refuse to paint *her* today.

The wind picks up and dark clouds cluster around the valley. The first drops of rain fall on my sketchpad, and it quickly becomes torrential. I gather my things and dash toward the house.

A child squeals with glee. I halt, glancing around for the girl to tell her to go inside before she gets too wet, but the gardens to the left and right are deserted. The child sings—a familiar tune, just out of reach of my memory. I scan the gardens again. She might be too small for me to see, but surely her parents are with her.

"Hello? Hello?"

Nothing. The rain thunders off the roofs, and I hurry inside. My clothes drip, my jeans cling to my hips. I discard them in the hall and run upstairs for my dressing gown. The air is cold for a moment, as though someone's opened the door.

"Hello?"

Silence. No door closing, no scurry of footsteps up the stairs. But I'm not alone. I sense someone watching me.

"Zenna?" Barely a whisper. I close my eyes and hold my breath, praying there won't be an answer.

There isn't. I let out a sharp gasp of relief.

And a door slams shut.

Rain lashes against the window and doors, battering the house all around. I'm on the stairs when Mum comes home, hugging my knees to my chest.

"Jo, are you okay?" She shakes out her umbrella and slips off her raincoat.

I hadn't meant to still be here like this. I should have been drawing or reading one of the books from her shelf or starting to prepare dinner. I hadn't meant to show my weakness.

"I was listening to the rain."

"It's passing over. Do you fancy another walk?"

We both change into dry clothes and when the clouds break and the sun re-emerges, we leave the house.

Past the wooden play park, past the Smugglers, the horizon is fuzzy and undefined—it's still raining out at sea. I watch the clouds unraveling into the water. Color has been washed away—the sea mirrors the melancholy sky. Everything is gray like my scrunched-up drawing from earlier. The headlands of Talland and Rame Head remain concealed by lingering mist. I tilt my head, embracing the soft sea spray against my face.

"We played here," I say.

"Yes, we did. You and me, a long time ago."

"No. Not with you ..." The thought melts away. I fumble for the right words then shake my head—it doesn't really matter.

A hand nestles into mine. Such a tangible sensation, I glance down to check, flexing my hand through my glove.

"The water's too cold to swim though," Mum says, as if I've caught the tail end of an entire conversation.

"I don't like swimming."

"Oh." She nods briefly, then abruptly strides away, crunching on the coarse, loose sand—her feet unstable as she sinks into it.

I hurry to catch her. The ever-changing beach becomes a band of colored pebbles, then damp compacted sand which preserves our footprints. I glance back at them, side by side yet so far apart.

"This is perfect." I turn to share my joy, but Mum's indifferent—her eyes hardened on the route ahead. I recall what she said about being used to it, about the beach being as ordinary as walking on a pavement.

It would never be ordinary to me. I'd sit here daily, capturing the vagaries of the seascape and the people. To the locals, I'd be as much part of the town as the café on the beach or the storms which changed the terrain so dramatically in 2014. I'd grow old here, in solitude and contentment.

Mum's ahead again. I run, *again*, to keep up with her, the way I did when I was little. She was always a fast walker; I was forever trailing behind while she urged me to *get a move on!*

Odd, these things surfacing, these obscure extracts. Is this how memories usually occur? Triggered glimpses into the past, sliding easily into place, without structure.

I extend my hand toward Mum—not to hold hers, but to visualize my six-year-old self clinging to her.

"Are you coming?" she yells, her voice drifting out to sea before it fully reaches me.

Further and further away. I don't rush. Soon, she'll be a dot, smaller than a dot, a moment of non-existence before we come back into visual range.

The cliff rises on my left, taking the road with it, up and over. The tide is going out; the beach widening with every passing minute. Waves tumble softly over themselves, a soothing swishing sound. I'm lulled, swaying, emulating the flow of the water.

A ragged band of rock protrudes from the sea—I played here, scrambling across them on lazy Sunday afternoons. *We* played. But I've forgotten who *we* were. I'm seized by an icy paralysis. Someone screams. But I'm alone. Water rushes around me, over me, as though I've fallen in. I'm struggling to breathe, floundering, splashing frantically. Rippled water shadows my skin.

"Jo, come on!"

I'm back on the beach, and the low gray cloud envelopes me.

The memory lingers, the sensation of drowning, the fear of it. Not as pronounced as when I fainted in the coffee shop, or the times since, when I've paused to allow the world to realign itself. I'm not *experiencing* it so much as recalling it. The emphasis has shifted.

"Hurry up," Mum yells, funneling the words toward me through her hands.

I drag my feet through the deep gravel, passing the rocks with a sense of foreboding.

A family is at the edge of the water. I watch them with fondness. A toddler and her dog splash in the waves and jump away. The dog gambols with excitement; the child darts forward to follow him. I tense, my eyes fixed on her, terrified for her. Her parents turn, distracted by their conversation. If she falls, they won't even notice. *I'll* know because *I'm* watching. I don't want to, but I must—just in case.

The girl laughs as the dog shakes sea water over her, holding out her hands to repel it. She topples over and lands heavily on the sand. She clambers to her Wellie-booted feet and wipes her trousers down ineffectively. She runs back and forth, jumping onto each little ripple as it reaches her, with exhilarated squeals.

I want to rush over and lift her up, to keep her from harm. I want to turn away, to pretend I never saw her and jettison my responsibility. Just in case.

I wait. Anticipating the very worst.

I want to shout out, to tell her parents they need to keep her close. A whimper escapes my lips.

"Jo, come on." Mum's beside me. She takes my arm to guide me away.

"That girl ..." My hand is limp as I point toward the shoreline. "She's too close. She'll be swept away. I don't like it."

"She's fine. See. Her dad is with her."

I cover my eyes. "She's going to fall in."

"No, she isn't. Her dad's holding her hand."

Mum lowers my hands from my eyes, and the girl's crouching, inspecting pebbles with her dad. She holds one between her finger and thumb for him to examine.

"It's okay, she's safe." Mum is directly in front of me, maintaining eye contact, turning me away from the water.

But it's not okay. I snatch glances behind me, adrenaline keeping me alert. My stomach churns with terror.

"They're walking back to their car." Mum steps back,

allowing me to watch the three of them plus the dog walk up the beach toward the car park. The girl holds her parents' hands and they swing her between them.

"Okay?"

I nod. My breathing slows. My shoulders relax. Mum releases her grip on my arm.

"Why don't we stop for a drink?" She points to the top of the cliff, up a steep set of steps, to the pub tucked right on the edge. "You look like you could use one."

I hadn't realized we'd walked so far. "Can we just go home?"

It's not safe out here anymore. Something's coming, something bad.

SEVENTEEN

Time is warping. It feels like minutes since I arrived in Cornwall, yet hours trying to get off this beach. Each step is a burden, pulling the weight of my terror. Hands wrap around my waist to prevent me. I haul myself forward, one slow encumbered step at a time.

The house is a sanctuary when we reach it. I press myself against the wall, enveloped by the painted woodchip. My dizziness intensifies and I want to be sick—heat rises within me, beads of sweat develop.

"Sit down. You look like you're going to faint."

"I'm fine." I fumble for the bottom stair and thump down onto it. I move further up, further away from the door—hunching over my knees, making myself as small as possible.

"Tea? Coffee?" Mum calls as she walks down the hall. "Something stronger?"

"I don't mind." It comes out as a murmur. The girl skips toward the water, heightening my vigilance. Hands tense, legs ready to run to her. I take deep, painful breaths, desperate to call out and stop her. She's in the water anyway. No one sees her but me. Only I can save her, but I'm too far away. I'll be too late.

"Here ..."

Did she get caught in the tide and swept out to sea? Or did

she walk away, like Mum said? I don't trust my memory—it plays too many tricks or evaporates altogether.

My hands shake as I take the wine glass from Mum. I'm foolish and ridiculous. My reflection is convex in the glass, my features distorted. I watch the wine shudder.

"Are you going to sit on the stairs all evening?" she asks.

"It's nice here. Safe."

"Safe?"

"Sorry. Don't mind me. I'm just a little ..." I let my words drift away and hope she wasn't listening. I can't explain; I realize my absurdity. Shivering under her scrutiny, I sip my wine and wish she'd go away.

"I'll get started on dinner. Is chicken okay?" And she's gone.

I remain on the stairs, doodling on a junk mail envelope left here. My hand dances over the marketing slogans. I capture the laden clouds from earlier, and the gentle waves lapping the sand—disconnecting, giving my subconscious free rein.

Mum peers through the bannister. "You've drawn the girl?" she says with surprise.

"Oh." I touch the page. I didn't mean to. I've drawn the angry sea swallowing her up, her parents frantically trying to reach her. It happened—I'm sure it happened.

We eat dinner with minimal conversation. Mum's distracted, focusing on her plate and pushing food around with her fork.

With every step forward, there are several backwards. We have nothing in common, no easy chatter. Mum offers nothing. She doesn't speak of family or friends; she maintains a wall around herself. She doesn't act like a mother should, like Nathan's mother—I'm closer to her than to the woman sat in front of me. If my children came home after a period of estrangement, I'd want to learn everything about them. I'd want them to feel they still had a place with me, that they belonged.

I'm a guest. We're on our best behavior. When I leave, we'll hug politely.

"Do you want to talk about what happened on the beach?"

"Not really. I don't even ... There *was* a girl? I didn't imagine her—you saw her too?"

"Yes, I saw her." She sets her knife and fork down. "I saw a toddler playing with her dog and her family. That's all it was."

"I know."

Just a child on the beach, like the thousands of children who play there every year; or the millions playing on all the beaches around the world without ever getting hurt.

"Are you married?" she asks suddenly.

"No. You think I wouldn't have invited you to my wedding?"

She smiles. "I'm sorry, of course not. It's just been so long—I don't know anything about you ..." She pauses and begins again. "What about a boyfriend? Anyone long term?"

"No. I'm happy the way I am."

"What about kids? Do you want kids?"

"I've never really thought about it. You imagine your future and sometimes certain things don't come up—for me, that's children."

She sips her wine and places the glass back on the coaster with utmost precision. "Is it my fault?"

"Why would it be?"

"Because ... I wasn't a ... *good* mother."

"You were a good mother. You were everything to me when Dad left." It seems like the right thing to say, but even with small memories returning, I don't recall the details of their separation. I don't know if it was acrimonious and full of spite, or if they drifted apart unable to reconcile some vital detail.

I wait because this might be the moment I get answers. Does she know this whole place is just a random seaside town to me, the landmarks and the people mean nothing? Does she realize she's a stranger—and why?

She finishes her drink, but she's disinclined to talk any more. Her expression alters, pushing aside whatever thoughts she was having. She gathers our plates, and I drain my glass.

I type "Jo Mckye" into the search bar, unsure what I'm seeking.

No, that's not true. I am sure: I'm searching for me. The real me. Not the shell. Not the empty vessel. I need to know who I was.

My name appears multiple times on the screen, but not all of the mentions are me. I scroll through—discounting the wrong ones—and click one for my university alumni page. There's a small biography, no pictures. It gives brief details, nothing I'm not already vaguely aware of. Nothing useful.

Digging further, I discover archived articles about the course, videos of our end-of-year exhibitions, and interviews with some of the students. A couple of names are familiar only because of their subsequent success; none of the faces are, except Spencer. Candid, behind-the-scenes photos without acknowledgement of who's in them form a decorative boarder. I scrutinize them, but none are of me.

Back to the search page, another result leads me to an art competition, with *WINNERS 2009* in bright blue letters across the top. In this, I placed fourth with an entry called *Girl and Rose*. Shivers cascade around my body. I don't want to click on the link. I don't want to know who the girl is. Because I already do. My hand is on the mouse. I click. The page loads.

Zenna smiles back at me. An unformed version of herself. Undeveloped. I don't recall the competition or the painting. Yet here she is, taunting me from the screen. Her hair is flowing across her shoulders, green in this picture. Her hair is never the same—it changes color and length, sometimes it hangs limply, at others it spreads out like the snakes of Medusa.

Her eyes are always the same—a curious shade of amber which doesn't appear among my paints. They shine as though caught in sunlight. The longer I stare, the more they penetrate.

"I'm going to the Smugglers," Mum calls up the stairs, and leaves immediately without inviting me.

I glance toward the door wondering what damage I've inflicted on our relationship this time, whether it's the beginning of another breakdown. It's all going wrong, and it's all my fault. I lean back against my pillows. Perhaps it's time to leave—I only planned to be here a couple of days, anyway. None of what I'd hoped for has occurred. I haven't salvaged memories or admitted my amnesia. The longer I'm here, the more time that passes, the harder it is to bring up—like answering to the name Jess because I waited too long to correct an acquaintance. It's sad, but there must be millions of people who don't get on with their family—I'm not the only one.

Remember me.

"Leave me alone. Get out of my head!"

A little girl laughs, and I'm chilled to my bones.

***

In the middle of the night, I'm wide awake. An owl hoots, foxes cry, something screeches further along the valley and makes me shudder.

I close my eyes and breathe deeply, evenly. Floating on the ocean, with Opera Pink mist swirling around me. To be more accurate, *over* the ocean—the mist holding me like a pair of hands. I drift to sleep, my lungs filling with crisp sea air.

Suddenly I'm thrashing against the waves. And Mum's with me, both of us frantic, immersed by the tide. I struggle to keep above the water, stretching toward the surface, gasping for air. The hands which kept me up now push me down—pressing firmly on my shoulders to prevent me breaking free, easing me toward my death.

I call for Mum, desperately trying to find her in the black, churned-up water. My lips are moving, my words reverberating around my head. But I can't hear my voice. In my head, I'm yelling, but the sound melts into the sea.

The hands loosen, and I wriggle away instinctively. I kick out and swim as fast as I can, swallowing water as I gasp with the exertion. I'm not moving. I'm stuck, tangled among the seaweed. Panicked and sinking as I flail. The hands are gone, but I'm going under.

At the very last moment, as I take my last gulp of air and expect to plummet to the ocean floor, all motion ceases. I'm in bed, flinching against the daylight; my arms are still trying to swim, my legs kick out. I'm bleary, as if I haven't slept at all. The dream crumbles; pieces ebb away as I grapple for them.

But it was more tangible than a dream. I was there. Icy water filled my lungs; my arms ached, and I watched my skin wrinkle.

Another memory? Did I almost drown, as a child? It could explain why Mum's so reticent to talk about the past. If she was responsible, and Dad blamed her for it, she might not want me around to remind her. If my calamity was the reason he left.

No, it doesn't make sense. He wouldn't leave me if he thought I was at risk. And Mum wouldn't push me away. She'd want to keep me safe; she'd hold me and vow never to let me go. If I had children, it's what I'd do.

None of this makes any sense.

I stare at the ceiling and watch the first fingers of dawn spread across my room.

EIGHTEEN

I message both Nathan and Lily over breakfast, a few back-and-forths of no consequence, which makes me feel calmer. I haven't meant to ignore them, but there's been little to say. My exhibition is going well—it will run for another week, Nathan says, and a couple more of the paintings have sold.

The longer I'm here, the further away London is. I can barely conceive my flat, my job, my life there. A barrier has grown around them, as though they're the nightmare and this tiny town is my reality.

Mum hasn't risen yet—indeed, I didn't hear her come home at all last night—but today feels different, lighter. I listen to every creak, waiting for her to descend. I eat my cereal and make coffee, and when I'm finished, I wash up.

Leaning against the wall, side-by-side, are three canvases—each primed with gesso and ready to be reworked. They weren't there yesterday.

"I finally remembered to pull them out for you," Mum says, striding into the kitchen. "I thought you might like to paint today. I'll be gone most of the afternoon, is that okay? I know I haven't spent much time with you, but ..."

I was ready for a showdown over how our evening ended, yet she's acting like nothing happened.

"No, it's fine. I didn't expect you to drop everything for me.

I'm the one who descended without telling you. Don't you want them for yourself?"

She shrugs. "I never got the hang of painting."

"The one in the lounge is good—"

"I got lucky. Have you eaten? Ooh, you've made coffee, how lovely." She maneuvers the conversation without me noticing. She doesn't mention last night, so I don't either—not even to ask if she had a nice time. Apparently, we're moving past it.

Once she's gone—downing her coffee on the way to the shower and grabbing a couple of biscuits as she heads out the front door—I set up the easel in the front garden. I prefer it outside; the house is unsettling without Mum's energy to combat it. The valley and the sea inspire the colors I squeeze onto the palette.

I hate the idea of reusing Mum's canvases. Mine are all stacked several deep against my bedroom walls, on top of the wardrobe, under the bed. Reusing them would make sense—for those which weren't quite as good as I'd hoped—but I need them. Along with my sketchbooks, they're my thoughts and memories at specific periods of time, my connection to myself.

It troubles me she didn't want to keep the work underneath. I regret not seeing it. It might have helped me make sense of her.

The weather has brightened; the sun is much stronger today, almost hot on my skin. The sky is Manganese Blue. Flimsy white clouds leave shadows on the hills as they sail past.

I wash the canvas with Hooker's Green and Gold and Cobalt Blue—breaking the scene into rigid blocks of color.

The outline of Zenna is apparent before I realize what I've done. Her sharp, elfin features follow. Her chin juts into the air, her glassy amber eyes pierce into the real world. I swipe my hand through the wet acrylic, and it smears.

"Hi there!"

I jump. The barman from the Smugglers—Craig?—is walking up the garden path, with a brief wave. I wipe my painted hands onto my jeans.

"Hello?"

"Mags asked me to bring you something for lunch from the pub." He presents me with a plastic-wrapped plate and laughs awkwardly.

Weird. Wait—Mags? What?

"Uh, thanks." I take it from him, not quite sure what to do next.

"Don't leave it too long. The quiche is nicer when it's hot."

"Cheers."

He hesitates, swaying on the spot but not moving. I glance at the plate in case he brought enough for two and is awaiting an invitation to sit.

"She actually asked you to bring me food?"

"Yeah. Well, it's what mums do, isn't it—fuss?"

I half-nod, half-shrug. I can't agree or disagree; I don't know.

Again, he doesn't move, and I'm not sure of the etiquette. I should probably make conversation, but I don't know what to say.

"How's it going?" He nods toward the canvas which, thankfully, he can't see. The long sludge of my handprint is beyond redemption.

"Okay. It's such a lovely place to paint."

"Perhaps I could commission something for the pub?"

"Maybe. Have you lived here long?"

"A couple of years." He takes a cautious step forward.

"So, you won't remember me like everyone else seems to?"

"No. But I've heard a lot about you. Your mum talks about you all the time."

"She does? You and Mum are ... friends, then? *Close* friends?"

He smiles and shoves his hands in his pockets. "Yes. Is it a problem?"

"Aren't you, like, my age?"

"I'm older than I look," he says carefully. "I'd better get back. Enjoy your lunch."

He ambles back down the path. It's none of my business—the mother I don't think about has a boyfriend I don't know about. It's good she's not alone, that my visions of her yearning for my return are unfounded. This bubble of resentment is ridiculous. I stab my finger into the quiche in vexation. It's hot; it burns.

After lunch, I return to the canvas and Zenna is remarkably intact, her colors matching the streaks on my jeans. I can't bring myself to erase her completely. She's morose today; her smugness and superiority replaced with something more wretched.

The surf is rolling in, white peaks blown up by the swelling wind. The ocean is endless, the sky expansive. If I painted nothing but shades of blue, it wouldn't be enough. I'm roused by the magnitude yet limited by the canvas.

In London, the relentless gloom presses against me. Even on dazzling summer days, the flat is dark and dreary. It shrinks as I think of it. The color of the walls escapes me; I don't remember if we have curtains or blinds.

"Have you finished?" Mum asks. She doesn't startle me as Craig did—her keys rattling in her hand signal her arrival.

"Not sure. It didn't go as planned. I can't decide whether to scrap it." I turn to face her. "You sent your boyfriend to check up on me."

"Oh, Craig? Just to bring you some lunch. I thought you could use a friend. *Boyfriend* is a bit ... not ... It's not like that." She flusters and holds out her hands to reset herself.

"Okay, yes. Craig and I are a ..." She scratches her head and frowns. "Not many people know. It's quite casual."

"Do you like him?"

"Yes."

"Love him?"

She smiles involuntarily. "Possibly."

"Then you shouldn't keep it a secret."

"So, you approve?" Her tone changes, deep and formal.

"If it makes any difference, I guess so."

She squeezes my arm. "Thank you. Can I have a look?" She points to the canvas eagerly, reaching it before I can answer. "Oh."

A clouded, troubled frown shadows her face briefly. She pushes a smile through her lips. Her hand follows the shape of Zenna's violated face, hovering inches from the wet paint.

"Well," she says, with a single clap. "I should get dinner started."

"Wait." I shake my head. "This is going to sound stupid. Do you remember my imaginary friend, when I was little? I called *her* Zenna, didn't I?"

"I think you did, yes."

Why didn't I remember this sooner? She was my constant companion, at one time. I made Mum set an extra place at the table and dish up a plate for her. When we went out, Zenna was always included, and Mum always had to help her put on her boots or find her coat. We spent a lot of time waiting for this invisible person to catch up with us.

All this dumps itself onto me, as if it's always been there.

I spin to face Mum, another thought pressing into me. "Do *you* recognize her?"

"Of course not—she's your imagination."

"But when you saw the painting just then ...?"

"You might have drawn her when you were little, I suppose. And she's in your exhibition. I was surprised you were still working on her." She picks at a stray thread dangling from her coat sleeve.

She's lying. She swallows and her face flushes. She fusses with my brushes and tubes of paint and avoids looking at Zenna. This is my chance to tackle her, to demand answers. But she goes inside before I get my thoughts in the correct order.

My imaginary friend? It makes sense.

A deep formative memory lurking in the recesses of my mind, despite whatever caused my memory loss; the comfort of childhood forcing itself to the fore.

"Yes, it makes sense," I say aloud, with only a bit of reservation. However, like Mum, I don't look at her again. I carry her inside facing away from me.

NINETEEN

The shower water runs blue then clear as I lather shampoo and wash paint from my hair. My body slowly warms back up—I hadn't noticed my skin mottling and my fingers growing numb. Mum suggests going to the Smugglers for dinner, but I plead exhaustion and change into my pajamas.

"Have you contacted any of your old school friends? Several of them are still quite local."

"I came to see you."

"You've only left the house twice since you've been home, and both of those because I made you."

"I'm recuperating. I was ill before I came down. It's nice to have some peace."

Just as it threatens to escalate into argument, Mum shrugs and continues her crossword, chewing the end of her pen. I pad around the kitchen, glancing at the already dark evening.

"How about I cook tonight?" I offer.

I rifle through the cupboards and ponder the almost empty fridge. I opt for cottage pie—minced beef, vegetables, mashed potatoes. I imagine it's one of the meals she made for me; an easy mid-week supper for a working mum to feed her active child.

Mum gives up her puzzle and pours wine, setting a glass on the counter for me. "I don't think you've ever cooked for me before—it's nice."

I smile feebly.

"I expect, being a famous London artist, you're rarely home to cook for yourself."

I laugh. "I'm a barista with a single, solo exhibition. Sometimes I can barely afford beans to put on my toast." I slice into an onion and blink back itchy tears.

"Really? I had no idea. Do you need money?"

"I'm exaggerating. It's not that bad yet."

"Your exhibition will help? You'll get more attention, more acclaim?"

"Maybe. But there are lots of us trying to make a living. Who knows if I'll be good enough."

It's not a consideration I usually allow myself—I've no idea why I'm being so honest. I ought to savor the idea of being famous, of being rich, of my art on display in Washington and Paris. This jaunt to Cornwall might be my Agatha Christie moment, discussed at every interview I undertake from now on.

"Anyway, I won't get anywhere if I only paint one woman for the rest of my career."

"It won't be like this forever."

"She's all over my older work too. In my sketchbooks ..." I stir the mince and gravy as it simmers. "In my uni portfolio. I googled it. I know."

Mum's hand trembles—she uses her other hand to steady the glass.

I drain the potatoes, mash them, assemble the component parts of the cottage pie, and put it into the oven. I lean against the sink, legs crossed at the ankle, glass in hand, and consider Mum carefully. She pretends not to notice.

"You didn't ask why," I say when her uneasiness is palpable.

"Sorry?"

"You'd think, wouldn't you, an artist would recognize her own work? Would know the pieces she put into her final uni portfolio? But you didn't ask why I had to search for it."

She sips her wine and straightens the placemat in front of her. She lays her palms and forearms flat on the table and shuffles in the chair. "No I didn't. Because I already know."

My heart skips a beat. "You know what, exactly?"

She exhales loudly. "You suffer from amnesia, and there's a good chance you don't remember growing up in this house, or me, or any of your friends from school." Her words tumble out in a steady, dispassionate stream.

"You didn't say anything."

"How would I do that, Jo?" Her sudden severity makes me jump. *"Hey, Jo. Nice to see you. I know you don't have a clue who I am, but hey—how are you?"* she says in an affected voice. "It was for you to make the first move, not me. It's not my responsibility."

She's risen in her seat—halfway between standing and sitting, her legs squatting to take her weight. When she realizes, she relaxes back into the chair.

It's almost dark. The hill behind the house is a tall, looming shadow; the sky embraces the last trace of sunlight. We're both reflected in the window, isolated and blank. I sit at the table opposite Mum, and she fills up our glasses.

"Is this what happens? We have stupid arguments and don't talk for years at a time?"

"Not exactly."

"Is it hereditary? Is Dad ... Is he not here because he forgot the way back?"

"No, no. That was something entirely different."

"I've been to doctors. No one knows what's wrong. They've

done MRIs and everything's normal. But it's not." I bite back my rage and accusations.

Mum folds in on herself defensively. She shrinks, becomes gray and mute in front of me.

The timer on the cooker dings, and we both jump. I smirk at my absurdity; Mum giggles.

As I stand, a bubble of water rises around me, swirling in my head, sucking oxygen from me. I gasp for breath, curling forward to steady myself against the counter. I'm underwater. Freezing. Caught in a tidal wave.

"Jo?"

"I'm fine."

Hands force me under ... I kick and panic and hold my breath ... It's not real. I'm in the kitchen. I'm safe. Arms restrain me.

I know you can hear me, Jo-Jo. I know you remember me,

"I remember you," I mumble. But it's not enough, or it's too late. She doesn't let go. "It's her, it's Zenna—she's here."

"It's just us, Jo." Mum presses her hand to my forehead. "No one else."

I twist around, checking for myself. Our reflections are distorted in the glass, against the dark backdrop outside. For a moment, a third figure hovers beside us. She leans over me, as if to comfort me the way Mum is. Our eyes meet. She vanishes.

"Zenna." I point to the window. "She was here. I saw her."

***

"We're going to the zoo, zoo, zoo," we sang. "How about you, you, you? You can come too, too, too."

It was something we sang wherever we went, substituting words as required. We went to the park for a lark, to the beach to eat a peach. *The shops* rhymed with *tops*, and we went to school because it was cool. I loved our songs; Mum didn't. She'd tell Dad to "Give it a rest, won't you?" through gritted teeth, and we'd quiet under her irritation. Dad would wink at me, so I knew it was him in trouble not me.

And so it happens, my father is fully formed in my head, crouched beside me because ... He fades and I'm alone. I was little, obediently waiting for him to tie my shoelace or zip up my coat. I hold my hand out to bring him back, but he's long gone.

On this particular occasion, it was just Mum and me in the car, so when I began to sing, I was subdued by her glare. I sank into the back seat so I could snarl at her without being seen in the rear-view mirror.

"Are we there yet?" I whined, my face pressed against the window as hedges and fields passed by, gazing up to the sky—making myself dizzy as the world zoomed along and my eyes couldn't take it all in.

"No," said Mum.

A little later: "Are we there yet?"

"No," she growled.

Later still: "Are we—?"

But her expression warned me off. It was funny when I did it to Dad—he laughed along with me and made up silly answers—but Mum didn't share our sense of humor. She was sad and serious most of the time, even when I tried to cheer her up. If I picked flowers from the side of the road, she'd say they were polluted and throw them away. The time I bought her a packet of giant chocolate buttons with my pocket money, I saw her furiously shoving them all into her mouth, when I was supposed to be asleep, then spitting them out into the sink.

Rage bubbled inside her, just under the surface, for most of my childhood. If I scratched her, I was afraid it would come tumbling out instead of blood.

We went to the train station, that day, the big one in Plymouth, with so many tracks I was always afraid we'd get lost.

We're going to the trains, trains, trains. We'll get wet in the rain, rain, rain.

We stayed in the car for a while, then went inside and sat on uncomfortable metal chairs on the concourse. We were waiting for a train, but we never migrated onto the platform to catch any of them. I dutifully noted each muffled announcement of trains departing to Bristol or Edinburgh or Cheltenham Spa—exotic places I'd never heard of—yet still we remained on those cold metal seats.

I glanced furtively at Mum, scared to complain I was thirsty and hungry. I sat with my legs swinging, gawking at the travelers sitting opposite me. Two students wearing too many clothes and one rucksack between them, straining at the seams; three women with shopping bags and a lot of laughter; a somber man in a suit reading the *Financial Times*. I didn't know it was the *FT* at the time—I thought it was a pretty color to make a newspaper from and must contain really fun news. I wondered why there weren't blue and yellow and green ones too, and if I should buy one for Mum.

At some point, she bought me a drink and a bag of crisps, but otherwise she sat rigidly, with her bag on her lap and her hands folded across the top of it. Her face was pale, like she was sick or she'd been crying, and she stared at the floor, taking no notice of me. I wanted to hold her hand, but there was space between us. I'd have had to move to the next seat, and she might have shouted. So, I waited patiently because I knew at some point something would happen.

It was getting dark outside. Not black like at night-time, but like when Mum tried to put me to bed after the clocks were put forward. Too light to sleep, but not daytime anymore.

"Stop fidgeting."

"Are we going to be here all night?"

The trains were fewer and less frequent. The shops pulled down their shutters, and the concourse emptied. Instead of the thunder of footsteps, single pairs of shoes echoed around the high ceiling. New arrivals—either from the platform or outside—passed through quickly and purposefully.

"Come on," Mum said finally, as my eyes were closing and my head lolled to one side. With a heavy exhalation, she stood slowly and stretched out. She held my hand as we walked back to the car.

We never talked about it. I forgot it.

I wonder if we were running away, or if she was planning something far worse. An icy finger slides along my body, all the way from my neck to my feet. Nathan was right—not all memories are good.

TWENTY

Mum says I'm depressed. She says withdrawing into my cocoon makes sense, if we think of it in that way. She says she felt the same when she was depressed.

It's not a conversation I relish having. I bow my head and blush.

She says she was sometimes so desolate she could barely move—she'd be walking along the road and suddenly stop, unable to find the impulse to continue.

"Is that around the time we went to the train station in Plymouth?"

She bites her lip. "You remember that?"

"Some of it." I hold her gaze.

"Yes, around then."

She says sometimes she saw things which weren't really there.

"Like what?"

"People," she says slowly. She closes her eyes and presses her forefinger against her lips. "Or perhaps they were real, and I was too isolated to realize." She rests her hand on my arm. "Is that how you feel?"

I flounder. I'm not sure.

No. It isn't. Of course it isn't.

Zenna isn't real. She never has been. She isn't baking

cakes for a charity sale; she isn't planning a night out with friends or gossiping on Facebook; she isn't out there somewhere in search of a new flat to rent. Because she doesn't exist.

The air is burdensome upon me, making my movements slow and arduous. Thoughts loop around my head without making sense, and I can't vocalize them. My attempts to consolidate them are tiring. Something's missing, always missing. I open my mouth to speak and burst into tears.

Mum tucks me up on the sofa, nestling me among the many cushions, wrapping blankets around me. She brushes a stray hair behind my ear and kisses my forehead. "Get some rest."

My mobile pings as I close my eyes—another message from Nathan. I drop the mobile to the floor without reading it. He's sent several today ... yesterday? Time is fluid, days are running from one to the next without me noticing. Hundreds of miles away, Nathan's an illusion. He, and London, no longer exist.

Is this what happens when people return home, no matter how long they've been away, as if the intervening time has no relevance? Many years, several months, or just a day or two—does it matter? Is there an intrinsic submissiveness to the person you were before?

In my mother's company, I regress. I'm seventeen again, twelve, eight. I'm not stopping. Four, three, two ...

My eyes close; my jaw unclenches, my mouth relaxes into an O.

There's a giggle.

We're going to the train, train, train.

My voice blends with someone else's, but it isn't Mum's. She's not singing; she's driving us to Plymouth. Her eyes are fixed on the road, her hands pressed into the steering wheel.

She glances at us in the rear-view mirror when she stops

at traffic lights. "Will you two shut up. I can't hear myself think."

"Aw, Mum ..." But it's not my voice. It's not me speaking.

I turn, but my subconscious prevents me seeing who's there—it inclines my head away or changes my perception, so this other person hides just out of sight.

***

I slip out of the house early. The streetlights are still on, but the birds are singing to greet the impending dawn. I wrap my coat around myself and wish I had gloves—crisp, biting mist blankets the valley, contrasting with the stuffy and oppressive house. I take a deep breath, and chill air glides through me, satisfying and refreshing.

I pass my car, abandoned and unused since I arrived, and drag my hand across the frost on the roof. It would be so easy to get in and drive away, return to London and all the tedium it provides. I pat the roof and walk away. Soon, but not yet.

The sea is serene, glass-like, slowly creeping back toward shore. There's no noise apart from my footsteps. Walking along the deserted beach is surreal. The moon tinges the air with silver, creating a haunting half-light. I've arrived in a softly-lit 1950s film noir.

My feet sink into the gravelly sand, crunching rhythmically with each laborious step; a hypnotic sound to quell my unease. Across the bay, from behind the cliffs and hills, the sun rises. A bouquet of scarlet and peach streaks across the sky.

Further along the beach, rocks bulge from the water, weathered and sharp. In a few hours, they'll only be accessible by wading or clambering over flatter, more colorful rocks which harbor pools of water and clumps of seaweed.

I back away, fearful of the waves enveloping me; afraid they'll seek me out and devour me. My chest tightens, the dread of the water rises again.

Remember!

She's abrupt and exasperated, as though I'm doing something wrong, not playing by the rules. I'm trying, but I don't know what I'm supposed to be remembering. My life is a series of distorted dreams from which I never wake. It's a silent film where I'm required to guess the plot. It's mid-way through a novel, yet I can't flick back to remind myself of the previous chapter.

The tide swirls closer, more ferocious. Splashing at my feet. I scramble sideways across the rocks to escape it, stupidly isolating myself, climbing higher as the water level rises. The sea crashes against the base, reaching further with each surge.

Remember me.

I turn quickly and my left foot slips into a rockpool. My ankle cracks; water leaks into my boot. "Shit."

A scornful laugh fills the air. The child from the rainstorm, from the café in London, from the reflection in the window. All of them Zenna.

"Tell me what you want."

She doesn't say anything. She's in my head, after all, my vindictive invisible friend, my deviant imagination. I laugh, but my hands are balled into fists. I miss a breath, waiting.

A dog yaps, and I'm on the shingle again. The sea is a long way off.

People swarm around me.

There are shouted *hellos* and *good mornings* crisscrossing the beach—a cacophony of noise rumbling around the cliffs.

Several of these newly-materialized dog walkers break their conversations to say good morning to me. They nod politely but eye me with the same apprehension Rose displayed on my first day, as though I've appeared in front of them from nowhere.

The beach café is open and early customers are already lining up. I head inside, in need of a soothing hot chocolate. "And a teacake, please," I add, reading from the menu at the side of the counter.

"You're Maggie's girl," says the waitress. It's not a question. "Staying long? Five-fifty, love."

"I don't know yet." I offer her a ten-pound note and keep my hand primed for the change.

"Why would you leave?" she says jovially. "It's perfect here."

"Yes, but I have a job to get back to."

"I bet your mum'll try to keep you."

I smile grimly. "Well, perhaps."

The conversation is left hanging as the woman turns to the next customer—an apparent regular, with a Jack Russell scuttling around his feet. When my order arrives, I take it outside to one of the picnic benches, where a low wall divides the café from the rest of the beach. I wrap my hand around my mug until the heat burns a little.

Between the screeching gulls, barking dogs, squealing toddlers, and general chatter, there are pockets of stillness when even the pitching waves cease. Mist tumbles across the village, smudging the lines between my dreams and the real world. The road vanishes behind it, the hills too.

Zenna is a pencil mark on the approaching horizon. She sits beside me with her chin resting on my shoulder. She dives from rocks. She's beside me and around me and seeping inside me. She's a dream and a memory and a fear. She whispers into my ear with increasing volume until the rest of the café is muffled. My dizziness returns, a momentary displacement.

Remember.

As distraction, I take my sketchbook from my bag and draw the beach. Beyond the mist, at low tide, it stretches for miles. At least, that's how it felt when I was six and how I draw it now—capturing the exuberance of skipping over the yellow-gray sand and jumping into the deep blue sea, the first icy rush of water on my feet and splashing against my legs.

Oh God—I'd forgotten. I used to swim. I used to play in the sea. I wasn't scared; I didn't recoil. When did it change?

When did the fear begin?

On the page, I add three people—elongated, misshapen figures with their faces obscured, the way shadows extend from their source on a midsummer evening. I like the detachment. They don't resemble people—I want them to be alien to me.

"You did cartwheels," I mutter without reason, swapping pencils and concentrating on the sky. "Every time your feet left the ground, you kicked sand into my face, and it blew into my eyes."

I pause, foolishly, for a reply. Because there won't be one; I'm sitting alone. Most of the other customers are sheltering beneath the lean-to. Yet, I sense someone—the proximity of someone breathing, the imposition of an arm pressed against mine. It's fleeting, but it leaves an additional chill against my side.

Summer-bronzed arms and legs, star-shaped, tumble over and over. Not my arms. Not my legs. I was a clumsy child, and these are graceful and sinuous.

"You tried to teach me, but I could never do them."

It was a game I played—my invisible friend was really my little sister. We bounced on my bed together, played hide-and-seek in the park, and rocked our dollies to sleep. I hugged her when the thunder scared her, and she took the blame for all the naughty things I did. We shared secrets. We talked about running away, but we never did.

I draw a series of the three characters in my sketchpad. My mother, myself, my "sister." They're abstract, at first, becoming more defined and tangible with each sketch. My mother, myself, Zenna.

TWENTY-ONE

Jo-Jo.

Her sudden arrivals no longer alarm me. She slips into the bed beside me, and I recall a thunderstorm where she was so very scared. Not her really, me. I was scared, projecting my worries onto this invisible person who I was able to soothe in my place.

There's no thunder tonight; the noises outside are more distant than usual. The foxes are quiet, tucked away in their dens against the freezing air. Even the moon is absent. In the speckled blackness, vague impressions of the room filter in.

"Come on," Zenna whispers. "Let's go for a swim."

The bed disappears beneath me, and I'm falling, tumbling. Plunging into a void without sides, without a bottom. I land on gray sand—not a beach, but inside my own painted version. Three shadowed figures face me. One of them approaches and holds out her hand to help me to my feet.

She laughs and runs. I race to catch up with her, and she turns cartwheels beside me. I try to copy, but my legs are unwieldy and graceless. At the edge of the water, she kicks off her shoes and tugs her t-shirt over her head.

"Are you coming?"

We're waist-deep before her sentence is complete. The

water surges and unbalances me. Zenna clasps my hand, preventing me from fleeing back onto the shore.

"I don't want to. I don't want to."

She laughs, breaking away from me and swimming a few strokes on her back; diving into the waves and re-emerging behind me.

"Boo!" She ducks under and jumps up.

I'm terrified every time she's out of sight. She dives again, and again, and again.

"Stop it. I don't like it," I plead, the briny sea masking my salty tears.

"Coward!"

She dives again. And again. But this time she doesn't reappear.

"Zenna? Zenna." Voice quaking, I dip down and stir my hands around the water.

She rises, triumphantly, several feet away; her arms and legs thrown up, somersaulting in the water with sheer joy.

Her face darkens, eyes widen. "Jo!"

She goes under, feet first, as though yanked from below. She doesn't emerge, and the water is agitated as she kicks and writhes against the unseen assailant. Bubbles dance on the surface as her breath escapes in measured spurts.

"Zenna!"

The water's completely clear, and she's vanished. I need to swim further out, in case she drifted away, but I can't. I'm frozen.

"Zenna." A whisper, a plea. *Come back, don't leave me here.* I've got to find her. I've got no choice.

Filling my lungs with air, I dive. I'm so far from shore, the beach is a pinprick. The sea's too deep for me to touch the bottom. I sink into the calm, turquoise ocean alone. I call out, and my voice carries for miles.

Mum's beside me. I sob, gagging on seawater, unable

to catch my breath. Residual panic compels me to keep searching. I endeavor to explain the urgency, to push Mum away so I can continue. Gradually, my surroundings reassemble themselves. My terror alleviates, my confusion dissipates.

Mum perches on the edge of the bed. Her hand hovers before brushing hair from my tear-damp, sweat-soaked face. I nuzzle into it. "Sssh," she hums.

How long has it been since my mother soothed me from a nightmare? I don't recall, but I imagine she must have done, once upon a time.

"I was drowning." No, that's not right. "*She* was drowning."

Mum sits up straight. "She," she repeats softly. She has tears in her eyes she doesn't wipe away. She smiles weakly and rests her hand on my arm. "Do you want to tell me about it?"

The images are fading. I don't know how to begin; I don't know how it started. I shake my head.

She kisses my forehead. "Get some sleep."

On her way out, she glances back and steadies herself on the door jamb. Silhouetted by the landing light, her expression is concealed, her body elongated.

***

Mum's already out when I get up. I didn't sleep for much of the night, scared of what I'd find lurking in my nightmares. I heard her alarm, and her padding to and from the bathroom, and up and down the stairs. I heard her gently tap on my door and ask if I was awake. I heard the front door close with a mixture of relief and trepidation.

Alone, but not. The house is restless; Zenna inside my head is excited and badgering. Her voice is a long, low grumble of thunder.

My vision is sleep-blurry as I scroll through my Facebook

feed to distract myself until I'm just re-reading the same posts over and over. I message Lily, but she doesn't reply—she's probably already at work. Nathan says: *Hey, can I get back to you? I'm at the gym,* but he'll probably forget.

I make myself a coffee and bring it back upstairs. On the landing, I stop at the closed door of the spare room—guest room, I suppose Mum calls it these days, decked out in neat but neutral furnishings, ready to be used at a moment's notice. Like mine was when I arrived. Perhaps she calls them *both* spare rooms.

We used to play in there—another space where we'd be out of Mum's way. Zenna would wait in the wardrobe and jump out to scare me. And when I yelled, Mum would tell me off.

"But Zenna did it," I'd wail, with the faith only a small child can achieve.

I turn the handle and push the door open. I squeeze my eyes shut, afraid of Zenna appearing in front of me—not the childhood invisible friend but the volatile accomplice of my nightmares, with her hair dripping with sea water, enticing me to follow her. The vague swell of water passes over me, the subtle dizziness.

The room is empty. The carpet is worn and sun-bleached; the curtains are thin and ugly. Only the tall mahogany wardrobe remains, the exact one where I played—the only item I hoped not to see ever again.

The hand which reaches for the handle isn't my bony, lined, adult hand. It's soft and plump, and the doorknob is palm sized. The wardrobe towers over me again—how young I was, how tall *it* was. It creaks and squeaks, and a child chuckles from inside. I fling the door open.

No one there.

Of course.

Just boxes. Stacked to the top, jammed together like a Tetris game; things without boxes slipped into the odd-shaped gaps. One of the boxes, which once housed a new DVD player, has my name written on the side in black marker.

I shimmy it out—Jenga-style—and, one by one, lay the contents across the floor. School photos, exam certificates in envelopes, reports right back to my first year at primary school, participation medals from various sports clubs. I touch each of them, as though memory through osmosis may occur.

In another, there are newspaper clippings with my name either in the headline or in the body text. They mention a career I don't remember, of selling art to a couple of A-list actors. Beneath it, a photo of Mum and me in front of a large painting—*LCCA, 2004, Untitled,* written on the back.

There's a brochure from my exhibition, the corner discolored and pulpy where red wine splashed on it. She was there! My estranged mother, who hasn't told me so herself, has seen my collection in London. She's been there. In London only a few days before I turned up on her doorstep, and she hasn't said anything.

I look again and flinch at the similarities between the painting and my dreams—I hadn't noticed before. Which came first, my nightmares or the rendering of them?

A larger box contains birthday cards and tiny boxes tied with ribbon labeled *First Tooth* and *First Hair Cut.* So many photos. I'm a baby with a shock of black hair, with bright red teething cheeks and a dummy. I'm walking tentatively, gripping my father's hand. I'm posing at the front door in a school uniform a fraction too big, my hair in tight, high bunches. At a party, on a beach, on Santa's knee. I recognize myself but have no attachment, no nostalgia for these captured moments.

I sit back on my heels and scan the boxes with incredulity. The breadth of memorabilia is astounding.

From the growing heap, I find a photo of Mum and me when I'm about five or six. She's so young, mid-twenties perhaps, but no older. She's holding my hand and beaming into the camera. She's being pulled out of the frame by someone on her other side. But I've only got half the picture in my hand—the edge is frayed, neatly torn. I don't know who's holding her other hand.

Mum fills the doorway and casts a broad shadow over me.

I show her the brochure from the Zenna exhibition. "You were in London?"

"You shouldn't be in here." But she kneels beside me and brushes her hand through the piles. She glances at the brochure, still held high in reproach. "I almost bumped into you. The next day, on my way to the station. You came out of a shop with a friend. I almost shouted out to you."

"Why?"

"Why did I almost shout?"

"Why were you *there*? Why didn't you tell me?"

"Oh." Yet again, she doesn't answer.

"What's going on? What aren't you telling me?"

"Oh, Jo—I wish ..." She glances at the wardrobe, at the mess I've made on the floor, and is suddenly gray and exhausted. "Okay," she says at last. "Okay."

She stands and lifts a box down from the top of the wardrobe, pushed back to the wall so I didn't even notice it. It's hefty, taped at the edges where the corners have torn. She brushes away the dust and peels back the flaps.

There are framed photos in this one. The first is of me and another girl, on rough sepia-tinted 1980s Truprint paper. We are sitting at the patio table, with colored beakers and plates in front of us, wearing summer dresses and squinting against the sun with big toothy grins.

Mum stares at the picture and wipes a tear.

I stare at the picture, at Mum, at everything spread across the floor.

And I remember.

Remember me.

I do. I do remember.
I had a sister. A younger sister.
She died.
She was Zenna.

TWENTY-TWO

Memories flood the room. My childhood unfurls in haste, hitting me, making me gasp.

I'm sitting for my GCSE Maths exam, on the hottest day of the year in the stuffy sports hall, nauseated because I forgot my water bottle and can't remember how to calculate the surface area of a sphere.

I'm watching *Dead Poet's Society* for the seventh time one Christmas, weeping at the "O Captain, my Captain" line. I bought the DVD for Mum because she loved it so much, and we saw it together the first couple of times. I'm obsessed with Robert Sean Leonard.

My parents argue downstairs, while I crawl into a ball and rock myself to sleep.

I'm painting. And painting. And painting.

I'm above myself, peering down. We're frozen, Mum and I— shifting from one reality to the next with increasing speed. Bombarded and battered. An avalanche I can't control.

I'm giving my mother a bouquet of flowers I picked from the side of the road on my way home from school. I'm huddled with extended family for a group photo at a fortieth birthday barbeque. I'm in the choir for the Christingle.

Memories. These are *my memories*. After so long living in a vacuum, they saturate me. I can't direct them, or conjure up specific events at will, or cast aside those I dislike. I'm a spectator.

Every walk to school, and argument with Mum, and juvenile joke. Playing rounders with friends, climbing trees, watching TV, and listening to music. Homework and sandcastles and being bridesmaid at Cousin Ruby's wedding. Sneaking home drunk, far too young.

The significant things mingled with the mundane, the poignant with the tedious.

And I'm painting, and painting, and painting.

"Stop!" I cry out when the persistent images consume me. But they don't.

They crash over me like the tide. They rain down on top of me until I can barely breathe.

Zenna's there, too—my baby sister, inserting herself into my life. Fighting for the remote control when I was watching *Art Attack*, stealing chips from my plate when hers were gone, blaming me for breaking Mum's favorite lamp. She's shouting at me or following me about. She's having a tantrum in the supermarket and making Mum cross; she's coiled on my lap, sucking her thumb.

She's a looming, evocative presence. A constant companion, until …

"Stop. Make it stop!" I cling to my mother, the way I did as a child.

It used to concern me how much of my life was locked up. I saw a therapist for a year or so, but it didn't work. I resented paying her bill; I should have been grateful.

How do people cope with so much inside them?

I'm rendered immobile by the deluge, pinned to the spot with the burden of it all.

There are simultaneous versions of my mother, all indus-
triously getting on with their day. A continual sequence
of placing plates in front of me, of firmly braiding my hair
before bed, of telling me off for a thousand different misde-
meanors. Images layering themselves upon each other like
cheap 1980s TV special effects.

Zenna's a baby, and a toddler, it's her first day of school
and she's proudly showing off her new patent black Mary
Jane shoes. She's spotty with chicken pox; she's putting a
tooth under her pillow. But she's not dead. I don't remember
the day she died.

"You were there," Mum says dolefully.

"You lied. I asked you who Zenna was. I *drew* her, and you
never told me."

"You drew a woman."

"No. Don't even."

"It's complicated." She's stricken, aghast; caught in a
moment she thought she'd moved away from.

It serves her right, for lying. She's put me through all this
when she could have told the truth. I stare bleakly at these
mementos scattered across the floor, my life packed away
into the wardrobe like unwanted ornaments and unused
tea-towels, and I think I hate her.

"I'm listening."

"We'll talk about it later, when you've calmed down."

"Calmed down! I'm not a child. You had no right to keep
this from me. I had a *sister!* I ought to know about her. I
ought to know why I can't remember her." I'm flushed and
furious. My arms wave uncontrollably and my voice rasps.
My thoughts tumble from my mouth until they no longer
make sense.

The obstacle, this thorny one I visualize between us,
becomes tangible and impossible. It expands, pushing us
further apart. The longer I remain in front of her, the more
repulsed I am.

I scramble to my feet and push her hand away from me. I rush from the room, from the suffocation of the house. I run and I wish I didn't have to stop.

TWENTY-THREE

The infernal mist cuts off the top of the hill behind Mum's house, fraying into it, leaving it unfinished. It's ceaseless, encompassing, ever closer.

My car keys are back in my room—I kick the wheel with frustration and grimace against the pain. How seamless would it have been to just drive, all the way back to London, right now? No emotion, no overwrought goodbyes. Maybe that's what happened before; maybe I already had my keys with me. I lay my hands on the roof and press my forehead onto the cold metal.

Dizziness returns. More concentrated than anything before. A shadow passes through me, chilling me from within. It's too much—too many emotions welling up, inflating inside me until I explode.

Mum's at the window like a ghost, like Zenna. Like all those paintings of Zenna when deep down I knew who she was but couldn't articulate it. Because I must have known, mustn't I? People don't just vanish from our lives; we carry them with us, we make them important because we remember them. Every single one of us, so essential to the world we inhabit. That energy can't just fade to nothing. We talk as though they're here, we tell each other little stories about them. Their existence and experiences are hoarded by those left behind, like exhibition pieces in a gallery.

Except I forgot.

I lurch toward the beach, encircled by dog walkers when I hit the sand. Their easy conversations drift toward me on the opaque air. One or two nod courteously, turning away quickly to avoid the requirement to speak.

Waves collapse against the sand, rolling onto the shore before the previous one abates, a thunderous collision. Something catches my eye, something red in the surf—someone in the water? In those rough waves, it's not safe.

Maybe I imagined it. I glance around to check if anyone else noticed. But they're focused on the beach ahead, or each other, or throwing sticks for their dogs to retrieve.

A dense knot swells in my stomach as I scan the water, adrenaline pumping.

An arm stretches out of the sea, waving at me. They're in trouble.

The swimmer bobs in and out of view. Blink, and they've gone. Blink, and they're back. I scan around for someone else to confirm what I'm seeing. No one's close enough to call out to; my words blow out to sea. I turn back, and the water's empty. Either I've lost my bearings, or they've ducked under again.

I wait for them to wave, or for anything resembling a person to appear. There's a gnawing ache in my chest, a grave foreboding. I jump up and down, trying to see further out.

"Hey!" I shout, accosting a couple walking past with a Doberman. "Is it safe to swim out there today, do you think? I thought I saw someone."

They glance over my shoulder toward the water, a cursory acknowledgement of my increasing alarm, then dismiss me with pleasantries and a shrug. They call their dog and hurry onwards.

But *I* can't walk away—I have to do something. I drop my bag on the sand and remove my coat, shivering as I acclimatize to the wintry air. I run forward, ankle-deep in the surf, and gasp—it's much colder than I expected. I attempt to keep my eye on the spot where I last saw the swimmer.

Further in, one wading step after the other. Slowing as the current pushes against me, as I become aware of how deep I'm going. Every part of me is solid and stressed and scared. The water's up to my knees. Further in, to my thighs.

"Hello? Hello?" I'm not sure if I'm loud enough. I strain to catch a reply.

The current's so strong out here, my whole body is involved with the mammoth task of each step. Up to my waist, my jumper heavy and billowing. My feet are numb, my fingers are cramped into tight claws. I slip on seaweed and lose my footing, catching myself before I fall.

I bend forward, peering through the murky, foaming surf. I barely see my hands as I stir them around in the water, hoping to brush against the swimmer, to catch a flailing arm or leg.

Still nothing.

They've been under too long. They'll be unconscious, or worse.

I have to check beneath the surface. I have to dive, to swim. I have to save them.

I lower myself slowly—my arms, my chest, my shoulders. Only my head is above the water, tilted to the sky, being sprayed. I jump back abruptly. Shivering, shaking. I can't. I can't do this.

If I don't, they'll die.

It's up to me.

But I can't.

I cry out with shame and anguish, the death of a stranger on my conscience.

"I'm coming," I yell, psyching myself into action. Simultaneously, a huge wave swells up and knocks me off my feet.

The bottom of the ocean is surprisingly calm, almost blissful. Bright sunlight sparkles on the surface and filters down, creating shadows on the golden seabed. Zenna's waiting for me. Dreaming, not dreaming; alive, not alive. I'm not cold anymore.

She watches me with glassy eyes, neither alarmed by my presence nor reaching to help me. She's exactly as I draw her—with sadness, with scorn. But there's something else. Gratification.

"You came for me," she says, with a reassuring smile.

"No, I ..." Perhaps I did.

I let my arms float away from me and my body sways in the ebbing water. My hair drifts around me, highlighted by the sun, like a mermaid. I glance at my legs, disappointed not to find a long, beautiful tail. I'm not breathing, but I don't have to anymore. The water gives me all I need.

"You think this is a dream." She laughs—the little girl giggle which follows me—joyous and animated. She strokes my cheek, and her hand is so tender, loving. Unlike the ferocity of previous encounters.

She raises her arms above her head and leans backwards until she's lying horizontally. She surrenders her body to a deep current which wrenches her away from me. Her face alters. No longer serene and beautiful, she's pallid and her eyes are dark, lifeless hollows. My own tranquility is broken, and my distress elevates. Without Zenna's protection, I'm drowning.

"No. Don't leave me!" But my voice is unheard, unspoken.

The sea is dark and dirty again. Crashing around me. I

thrash, kicking, wrestling my way to the surface against robust waves. Icy water fills my lungs in rapid gulps. My muscles are weary, my resolve falters. My arms twitch ineffectually. I descend. Eyes open, I watch the surface get further away.

I'm wrenched up, out. Warm arms cradle me, and I'm flung onto compacted sand. I gasp, grappling for oxygen, but my lungs are solid and deflated. Hands pound my chest. Warm air is thrust into my throat.

"Jo! Oh my God, Jo!"

Craig. His face is close to mine when I open my eyes, smiling reassuringly although his eyes are serious and scared. I try to smile back, but my body is disconnected, and I can't be sure I've made any movement at all. It was cold a moment ago, now I feel nothing. My vision flickers, and Craig starts to recede.

"Stay with me, Jo," he murmurs. "The ambulance is coming."

And everything is black.

TWENTY-FOUR

I'm in bed with a cannula in my hand and a tube attached to a drip dangling above me. The tape keeping it in place is itchy, but I can't coordinate my other hand to scratch it. The machine beside me beeps merrily, and shoes squeak on lino along the corridor. Opposite my bed, a gray-haired lady's muttering about daffodils in her sleep, and at the nurses' station, several phones are ringing at the same time. Mum's dozing in the chair beside me.

My whole body is battered and swollen; my lungs are tight as I breathe. I groan as I use my elbows to prop myself up, and my head throbs. Mum stirs.

"You shouldn't be moving. What do you need?"

She reaches for a beaker before I reply, and I swallow thick, tepid water uncomfortably—allowing her to support the weight of my head. I slump back onto my pillow.

"How are you feeling?"

"Sore." My voice is whisper-weak. It scratches against my throat. "Hungover." Hungover isn't right. I wasn't drinking.

"Do you remember what happened?"

Hazy, fractured moments pass in and out of my head. None make sense, until ... "You lied to me."

"It's not that simple. But it's not what I meant." She squirms as I watch her. "We'll talk, when you're better."

"Yeah, sure we will. Because we talk so well."

I turn my head away from her. There's not much of a view—I'm facing the window, but from this angle all I can see are stark branches of a tall ash tree bowing in the wind and the winter-laden Naples Yellow clouds beyond.

The chair creaks as Mum shuffles to get comfortable. I imagine her leaning forward with her elbows on her knees, pondering what to do next. Is she staring out of the window too, sharing this same moment? The tree is resilient and majestic, here long before any of us, witness to the loves and losses of so many who've sat beneath it.

Fragments of memory break through. Bouncing on a trampoline when I was six, my first day of uni, the day in the railway station with Mum, eating ice cream after a harrowing dental appointment. These moments disperse before I can grab them, like reflections on a rippling pond.

"Well, I suppose I should go, let you get some rest." She bends over me to kiss my cheek and her scarf tickles my face. "I'll be back tomorrow."

A robin lands on a branch, gathering strength in its tiny wings before flittering off again. I listen to Mum's echoing footsteps halt and the solid door at the end of the ward slams shut.

With my next blink, I'm walking on a beach as the sun sets. Zenna's beside me, a shadow or a ghost. Every time I glance across, she becomes transparent. But she's still there, I hear her soft breath as if it's the wind. She's playing with me.

The sunset is animated in pastel, pink and lilac and orange merging together—one of my doodles from a few days ago. I've fallen into my own art, enveloped by the pages of a book. Zenna simply smiles.

We walk. Sometimes we're side-by-side with matching strides; at others, the length of an infinite beach is between us. Days and days pass. So many of them, they've assembled into weeks and months and years. I grow old, while Zenna stays the same—an age she never achieved in life. My hair is slate gray and bristly, my face wrinkled and leathery, while she is fresh and incandescent. She giggles and skips away.

The machine beside me beeps. Shoes squeak on lino. Several phones ring at the same time, and Craig appears at the foot of my bed.

"The nurse said you were awake," he says apologetically, once my eyes are open enough to focus on him.

"I was just dozing." Memories, thoughts, all in the wrong order. "You rescued me, didn't you?"

He nods. "I was on my way to work. In the right place at the right time, luckily."

"Thank you."

"How are you feeling?"

"Sore. A bit confused. There was a swimmer ..." Foggy, soggy memories.

"It's not important."

"I couldn't find him." I try to sit up, agitated. I need to find him. "Is he safe? Did you find him? Is he okay?"

"Jo, don't worry—"

"I need to know he's all right."

Craig pulls on his chin. "You should really talk to your mum about this."

"I don't want to talk to her at all."

His face contorts, as though he's having a soundless conversation with himself. His eyes dart, his mouth twitches. "I don't think there was a swimmer. There was a witness who said you just walked into the water."

"No, I saw him. He was waving, and I couldn't find him." Tears run down my face, past my ear, onto the pillow. "I was looking. I couldn't ..."

"They said you took off your coat and waded in."

No. There *was* a swimmer. He was in trouble. He was waving.

"I'm sorry—I shouldn't have said anything."

"No, I'm glad you did." The red speck dips in and out of the water. It did. I know it did. "I can't handle anymore lies."

He glances away, and our previous awkwardness returns. "I should let you rest. I wanted to make sure you were okay." He half-nods to himself as confirmation he's going, or that I am indeed okay, and moves toward the door.

"Craig?"

He pauses.

"I didn't mean to be rude, the other day. I was surprised Mum didn't mention you, that's all. I'm glad she's got you."

He nods again. "I'll see you soon."

As he leaves, I imagine it's Nathan walking away with promises to return. Nathan who I wish was here more than anyone else. I need his kindness and strength, his cheerfulness and unwavering friendship. I need his warm kiss on my forehead and his strong arms around me. Without my memories, I've always considered myself alone. But I'm not—I never have been.

Nathan would pause as he rounded the corner; he'd wink at me.

I should phone him, tell him what's happened. Instead, I allow my eyes to close—the exertion of being awake is too great. The pain medication eliminates the voices in my head and quells the images. The peacefulness is a relief.

***

The doctor discharges me into Mum's care, with the understanding I remain with her to rest and recover. Mum is attentive as he explains the symptoms and relapses to be aware of; she asks questions to clarify one point or another.

When the doctor leaves, the strain between us is an insurmountable brick wall. We haven't talked since yesterday. In front of the doctor, we focused on him.

"I'll phone Nathan. He'll drive down and take me home," I say, while Mum neatly folds the clothes I drowned in.

"Don't be silly. You can't go anywhere in your condition."

"He'll be here by this evening." I continue without hearing her.

"Jo, stop it." Her lips purse, as though fighting to prevent further words spilling out. Her loving façade is faltering. She zips up my bag with finality.

On the way home, Mum fiddles with the radio and the mundane babble of the BBC 4 host fills the space. I lie back against the headrest as hedges flash past. I open the window and inhale the musky odor of manure and damp grass. The motion of the car rocks me into a soft slumber.

Mum is steely and precise as she drives; her knuckles are white where she's gripping the wheel. I wish I had my paints, to capture her fragility and anguish, to remind myself of her grief. Yesterday, she almost lost a second child. And I yelled at her.

Still, we don't talk.

She tucks me in on the sofa, plumping the cushions and fussing over the curtains and the angle of the TV. She's in and out of the room with sandwiches and extra pillows and glasses of water so I can take my medication.

Occasionally she pauses and covers her mouth with her hand as though to subdue a sob.

TWENTY-FIVE

All the versions of Mum trapped in my head, all my memories of her, fill the kettle and click the switch. They splinter to load the washing machine or hunt for snacks. The real one pulls out a packet of chocolate chip cookies— she believes she can pacify me with the *good ones* she keeps for special occasions. They all stir the teabags in the mugs, awaiting the right depth of color before adding milk.

"You shouldn't be up," the real one says without turning. "The doctor made me promise you'd take it easy."

I slump against the wall, exhausted and overflowing, everything all at once. "I'm bored."

She brings the mugs to the table and sits. I do the same. "You were never good at being ill as a kid, either. You'd want to play with toys or scamper around the garden. I had to rein you in."

The knowledge is wedged into my head. I don't need her to tell me. People do though, all the time—they tell each other what they already know, confirming their own recollections match everyone else's, filling the spaces between sentences. I'd never really noticed it when my own gaps were so cavernous.

We drink our tea and eat cookies. I nibble around a large chunk of chocolate, carefully removing the biscuit before holding the chocolate in my mouth to melt.

"You used to do that too." She tries to smile, but it vanishes, leaving her lips oddly curled. She crosses her arms on the table and leans over them.

"I remember the day you were born. It doesn't seem so long ago—time plays tricks." She smiles wistfully. "I remember cradling you to sleep—you'd snuggle under my chin and hold onto my earlobe to comfort yourself."

I don't care. I don't want to know. I look over her shoulder her at the tap dripping steadily like someone knocking on the window to come in.

She takes another cookie and breaks off a small piece, examining it rather than eating it. She drops it back onto the plate.

"When you were two and a half, I had another baby. We named her Selena. You couldn't say it properly—it came out as Zenna instead." She dips her head and peers at me, checking that I'm listening.

"I asked you who she was. You let me make up all kinds of fantasy, and you hid her away in a cupboard."

She inhales and puffs out her cheeks. "When I saw your exhibition, I knew it wouldn't be long before you turned up here again."

"Again?"

She holds up her hand to hush me. "I have to explain this my way."

Déjà vu sweeps over me. I fold my arms to protect myself.

"You loved her so much. You took care of her, wouldn't let her out of your sight."

"She was like a little doll ..." I whisper.

"You used to call her *my Zenna*."

"My Zenna ... I remember." She's in her cot and I'm lying on the floor beside it while she gurgles and kicks off her blankets. I'm keeping her safe because Mummy's busy. "I'd pretend to be asleep, so you'd carry me to bed, like you did with her."

Mum pushes her chair from the table and reaches for a box on the floor beside her. When she puts it down, its heft shakes the table. She opens several Truprint envelopes and spreads the photos across the table like a deck of playing cards. *Pick a card, any card.* There are hundreds of them— of me, Dad, Mum, Zenna. Snapshots of my life, of *our* lives all together.

I was a cute kid, with dark ringlets and a cheeky grin. Zenna was *beautiful*. Blonde and wide-eyed, as if in awe of everything. She was porcelain and delicate. There was always something lurking below the surface, something spiteful—a pinch on my arm the grown-ups didn't notice, my favorite doll mutilated. When I portray her adult persona, I capture the embryonic menace of these early years.

There's no order to them. We grow and shrink, age and return to babyhood with a flick of my hand. I pause at one of all four of us at the zoo, in front of the lion enclosure with cheap plastic sunglasses and ice-cream grins. A willing passerby must have taken the picture so we could all be in it together. Behind us, a lioness paces, stalking.

I touch Dad's face. He's crouching a little, so he doesn't tower over us—knees bent, one hand on his leg for support, the other around Mum's shoulders. His smile is a laugh not quite realized. He's still just a hole in my memory, a trick of the light, a glimmer in the distance. His features morph until he's a stranger again.

"He left when you were ten," Mum says tersely.

I won't get any more information from her—her resentment is deep set. But I don't think I need it. Instead I turn to a photo of Zenna alone, with the furred edge of being torn off. It's the other half of the one upstairs. I was pulling Mum one way; she the other.

"I still don't know how she died. I've remembered so much—I don't understand why this is so hard."

She takes the photo from me and smiles sadly. "You were nine. She was ... six. There was an accident." Her voice cracks. "Zenna drowned."

Her sobs are deep and raw as she runs from the room, hand pushed against her mouth. There's a blast of air as the front door opens and slams shut.

I remain at the table, fumbling through these ostracized pieces of my life. We were happy, laughing into the camera; normal family life captured so we didn't have to remember. Yet, a couple of months, a couple of years later, we were fractured.

So many questions bounce around my head. Why all the secrecy? Why are these photos in a box, tucked away where no one can see them? Why aren't they displayed and honored? What else happened?

Other people have lost siblings; other people haven't misplaced their memory because of it. In my head, Zenna's still alive. Her death is a mystery—concealed, out of reach. I can't visualize it the way Mum can.

Mum returns, leaning against the door jamb with a vacant, drained expression. Broken, like me. Like Zenna. Tormented and unraveled, disappearing in front of me. I rush forward to save her from collapsing. Our arms tangle into an embrace, and she rests her head on my shoulder. She's wearing the same perfume she always has, the fragrance warm and soothing as it mixes with nicotine. She shudders as she cries, and I move away.

"There's more, isn't there?"

She nods, mouthing words under her breath. I lean in to listen. "I can't, Jo ... I'm so tired. I thought, this time—"

"This time?" I laugh scathingly. "Nothing changes, does it? You sound like you're giving answers, and suddenly there's a whole lot of other shit you're still hiding. She's *hurting* me. She's burrowing into my head and won't leave me alone."

I bang my fists against my temples. I want to do the same to Mum, so she'll bear the same pain.

"Stop it, Jo. Please."

"She's everywhere—forcing herself into my work, my life, my nightmares. And I don't understand any of it." My voice rises until it hurts. "I almost *drowned* because I thought I saw someone in the water. But it was her." I stop abruptly, the force of this latest truth settling on me. "It was her."

We stare at each other in horror and comprehension. Fingers of cold air swirl around us.

TWENTY-SIX

Pencil poised over my sketchpad, I'm scared to make the first mark, scared the mark will be Zenna.

Everything Mum showed me yesterday remains scattered about the house, in the spare … in Zenna's room and across the kitchen table. I brought some of the photos into the lounge once I'd put Mum to bed and sat with a glass of wine remembering the real Zenna, not this cryptic creature of my imagination.

Mum's still upstairs, sleeping after a disturbed night. I woke too early, long before dawn, tossing and turning as my past nudged itself into its rightful place.

The pencil remains above the unblemished page.

The weather's turned; frost covers the ground and hangs from the trees like tinsel, casting an ethereal presence over the valley. Zenna passes behind me, sweeping a draught along with her, but when I turn, the room's empty. As it should be.

A child laughs.

"Stop it," I say sharply, then cover my mouth to keep the noise from waking Mum.

A cold arm reaches around my shoulder. My feet are wet. Water rises. Up my legs, so my pajama trousers billow and my dressing gown floats around me. To my torso and chest and throat.

It's time.

"Leave me alone, it's not fair."

And I'm drowning again.

Struggling against the tide. Fighting to keep myself above the rushing ocean.

It's not real, it's not real, I chant silently. Not real, not real.

I take a final breath and hold it as the oxygen depletes, as my body fills with water. As Zenna's terror is injected into me.

The red and peach smudge of sunrise fills the space between wakefulness and my dream. Water ripples tranquilly; warm sand oozes between my bare toes.

I'm not afraid. I was, once. Yesterday? The day before?

You remember me.

You remember ...

"You remember me." Her voice extracts itself from my head, and it's in the room, as palpable as I am. The body it belongs to sits beside me. The sofa dips, and I tip toward her.

"Zenna."

"Oh yes, and you're my Jo-Jo. At last. I've missed you so much."

"You're not real. You don't belong here anymore."

Her radiance falters—the air around her grows darker. "That's not true."

No longer a hallucination, she glares with corporeal eyes on her corporeal face. She takes my hand in hers with an impish smile. Her lifeless fingers transfer their chill along my arm, penetrating my bones. I'm solid, unable to snatch my hand away.

The room disintegrates, splintering my life out into the universe and sucking it back in. When it's repaired, we're on the beach.

"It's just a dream," I mutter. "I'm at home on the sofa.

Mum's upstairs. I'm dreaming and Mum's upstairs. I'm dreaming and Mum's ..."

The sea is inky, almost inert against the shore. A cool zephyr brushes against us, causing our hair to flutter around our faces.

"We should walk for a while, like we used to," Zenna says, taking my hand. It's the hand of a child, small and delicate in my own adult one.

"I don't remember."

She's still jumbled up to me. I recall snippets of us together, but she's on the periphery. My other memories are a constant slog, playing over and over. But not Zenna. She's trapped between worlds, hidden behind paint on a canvas, trying to scratch herself out.

"You really should stop saying that," she says lightly. "It's not that you *don't* remember —you choose not to. It's too hard, I understand. After all, you did a terrible thing."

I pull my hand away from hers. *A terrible thing?*

Zenna smiles reflectively. "Come on. I want to show you something."

She glides over the beach rather than scrambling through it like I do. My footprints create a solitary line.

"Where are we going?" I struggle to keep up with her. The faster I go, the more my feet sink into the damp sand.

She stops abruptly and points without a word. I gaze into the expanse of Winsor Blue sea, uncertain where I should be looking. A pitted rock protrudes from the water. I glance back at Zenna, and she nods.

"That's where I drowned," she says simply. "Just off the rock there."

Her words hang in the air between us. I close my eyes and try to remember.

For a moment, it's dark. Then the sun is shining, warming my face. Not risen, just there, as though it has been all along. With it, the golden haze of a hot summer's day, and profound, rapid excitement rising within me. Children laugh and shriek; dogs bark, zealously chasing balls. Basking tourists provide a hubbub of chatter, the soundtrack of my summer holidays. I burst with the thrill of my tiny village swelling with all these new people.

Zenna jumps around beside me because we're young again, although I'm not sure how young. Zenna still possesses the cuteness and plumpness of a preschooler. People tell her she's pretty and delightful. Then they turn to me—gangly and gauche beside her—and their smiles quiver for a fraction, before they regroup and call me *lovely* as if it's a question.

It bristles. I narrow my eyes and become surly. I hate them comparing me with my perfect little sister. It burns, yet she basks in the adoration—why wouldn't she?

We run to the edge of the water together, and my resentment is forgotten because it's a hot, sunny day and we're playing. We splash into the surf, wading until it reaches our knees, our thighs. Mum's warnings to *be careful* ring in our ears, but today, we're invincible.

Waist-deep, we belly flop forward, submerging ourselves and leaping out with loud yells. Over and over, swimming back and forth between the flags until we flop onto our towels with exhaustion.

Mum doles out egg sandwiches, and we buy ice creams for dessert. Afterwards, we play football—Mum's drilled into us not to swim directly after we've eaten. With every kick, we glance across for her approval. *Mum, look at me, look at this!* Some kids we met earlier in the week join us while their parents pack up their picnic stuff. Mum's lying on the blanket, with her straw hat tilted across her face for shade.

The afternoon passes. The sun moves across the sky and the crowd begins to dissolve. As the water empties, we dive back in. It almost feels warmer than it was earlier—a day's worth of sun has heated it to perfection. The people leaving now are missing the best part. The beach is quiet, and people stroll idly with their dogs panting contentedly beside them. The waves are crinkles in the clear water; the sun is Gold Ochre.

"Girls, it's time to go," Mum calls.

"Just a little bit longer," we wail in unison. And she indulgently relents.

"Half an hour, then, but *no* more."

I float on my back and allow myself to be shunted by the tide. Wispy clouds drift above me. Zenna's beside me. Until she isn't.

I jump to my feet and scan the water, then the beach. She's over on the rocks, clambering to the far side, where the seabed drops away and the water is much deeper. I can't find Mum in the blemishes of color on the beach, which means she probably can't see Zenna.

Zenna holds her hands above her head, preparing to dive.

"No!" I yell.

We're not allowed to do that—it's dangerous because of all the hidden rocks beneath the surface. *You could break your necks*, Mum tells us, time and again.

Zenna can't hear me, or she's ignoring me. I swim across, but the tide pushes against me, deceptively strong just this tiny bit further out. It pushes me away from her. I call out again, to Zenna, to Mum, to anyone at all. Zenna spots me and waves. She smiles and dives.

I almost swallow water in my effort to reach her, soaring through the surf, using every bit of strength I have. Head down, I attack the water. Each time I check my position, Zenna's further away. I'm losing power, my arms and legs becoming less effective as I yield to the weariness.

Eventually, finally, almost not-quite, I grab her leg.

She's bleeding. Her head is cut. She's under the water, and her eyes are open. I try to haul her up, but she slips from my grip. I hook my arm around her and try to swim. She's too limp and heavy.

I can't do it.

"Help!" I scream. "Mummy!"

Slowly, people come running. I spot their brightly-colored t-shirts first, bounding across the beach, then hear the yelling. Several people wade toward us. My arm is tingly with pins-and-needles, and Zenna's face is barely above the water. She continually slips away from me, while tears stream down my face because I'm petrified I'm going to drop her.

They wrench Zenna from my arms and rush to the sand, lying her down and performing CPR. Many voices fill the air, calling for help. Someone runs to the payphone.

A woman asks, "How long has it been?"

I can't take my eyes off Zenna's floppy blue body. The question hangs in the air.

"How long was she under the water, love?" she repeats, firmly, crouching to block my view of the beach and Zenna and the flock of bright t-shirts gathered around her. She shakes my shoulders to elicit a response.

"I don't know. I don't know!"

I have no idea how much time has passed, is passing. I fix on Zenna's pale, lifeless face, and the man knelt beside her blowing air into her lungs and pumping her chest up and down.

The woman hugs me tightly, wrapping her cardigan around my shoulders.

And Mum screams.

TWENTY-SEVEN

"Of course," says Zenna, here and now—fully grown, although she never was, never will be, "that's not what *really* happened."

We're apart from the crowd, sitting side-by-side and observing the commotion.

The child Zenna is lying on the sand and my nine-year-old self is being restrained by the stranger who's trying her best to shield my eyes. The efforts to save her are no longer sincere, they're actors playing a part—Zenna's magic conjuring up a replay.

"You held me under," she says without emotion, still fixed on the scene in front of us.

Mum—or, at least, a two-dimensional version of her—rushes across the beach, with her blood-chilling scream. I remember the scream. The sound resonates through me. She slithers to her knees beside Zenna, collapsing over her cataleptic body, embracing her with such a wretched wail. It's already too late—*she* was too late.

"I thought it was a game," Zenna says. "I trusted you. But you wouldn't let me go."

Mum's still on the sand, pushing away any attempt to comfort or contain her. She strokes her baby's face, brushes away the sand which has gathered on her hairline, rocks her, sings a lullaby. I squeeze my eyes shut and push my hands against my ears.

"You killed me, Jo-Jo. You were supposed to look after me, and you killed me."

And now we're in a different version.

We're *both* on the rocks. Zenna's messing around, balancing on one leg and pretending to tip over, and I'm encouraging her.

"I'll give you my sweeties if you dive in," I say in Zenna's voice, horrible words wedged into my mouth. "I'll give you my best dolly. I won't tell Mummy."

And she almost does but catches herself at the last moment. She teeters, overbalancing. I nudge her. A tiny prod, that's all it takes. She tumbles and hits her head. And she bleeds.

I scramble down after her, cutting my leg on the rock, and it stings as the salt seeps into it. Zenna's under the water, not even trying to get up. Her hair floats around her; her face is serene, like an angel. Her eyes are open, but unresponsive. I press on her shoulder, restraining her, resisting the buoyancy of her body. Her blood flows crimson into the sea, sharing itself with all the oceans. I laugh.

But it's not my laugh. It's Zenna's, cruel and unflinching. Gradually the vision fades, and it's just the two of us again, on the vast expanse of an empty beach.

Zenna drags me to the water. She grips my jaw and forces me to face the murky surf. She tightens her hold, until I'm pinned against her, and coerces me closer to the edge. I writhe and wriggle, digging my heels into the sand, frantic to break free. The tide laps our toes. Her eyes are fiery, her face harsh and menacing. She's stronger than me. She lifts me from the ground, my feet kick in mid-air.

"No! That's not what happened!" My voice falters: I'm moving my lips long after the sound has diffused.

I twist, scream, kick out, strain to bite her so she releases me. She's firm and unyielding.

"It's your turn, *Sister*."

I push against her, leaning back to make my body as cumbersome as possible. She can't get purchase. I jolt back and forth, with as much weight as possible, and slide from her grasp. I sprint into the darkness, along a coast which is no longer there.

The real world trickles back in various shades of gray. The room is fuzzy, and my vision impeded. I flinch against the burning daylight.

"Jo. Jo? On my God, Jo ...?"

I'm back in the lounge, sprawled on the floor. My arm is uncomfortable beneath me, with pins-and-needles digging into it. Mum hauls me into a sitting position, but I collapse against the sofa, disorientated and detached.

"Jo, can you hear me?" She taps my cheek, leaning over me, her face etched with terror. "Talk to me."

The urgency in her voice frightens me. Her anguish is a reprise of when she saw Zenna on the beach. My mouth opens, but the sounds are vague and unformed.

"Zenna," I manage at last and it consumes all my energy.

"Oh, thank God." She folds me into a hug; I allow my head to rest against her shoulder.

The haunting, lingering image of Zenna on the sand persists.

"What did I do?" I whisper.

Mum extracts herself from the embrace. "Come on, let's get you comfortable." She helps me up onto the sofa, and I flop in an uncooperative heap. She tucks a blanket around my torso, and the warmth slowly radiates into me.

"I had a dream—"

"You scared me. I was about to call an ambulance. I thought ... Perhaps I still should." She chews on her lip, frowning with concern. She glances between the phone and me several times. "Or, at least, the doctor. Am I blurry to you?" She holds up one finger and moves it across my field of vision. "Follow my hand."

"I was on the beach," I say. "With Zenna. She jumped, from the rocks. No, I pushed her. I *killed* her." I grab Mum's hand. "It was my fault. I had a sister and I killed her."

She shakes her head, pushing my words away as though they're not important. She isn't really listening—she's reaching for the glass of water I filled earlier and pressing it to my lips.

"She showed me what happened. I remember it."

"It was just a dream. It's not what happened."

"I felt it." I'm nauseated as I relive it. Zenna's inert face below the surface, just like my painting of her. *Zenna in the Sea*—that's what I called it. I knew. It's always been inside me.

Mum shakes her head, so forcefully her shoulders follow. "No, no, no," she murmurs.

I need the truth. "Did I do it?"

Did I do it?

Such a simple question, and yet such an immense and inflamed one.

I'm not ready for the answer.

Mum draws out a long, deep sigh. She strokes my cheek, and a single tear slides down her face. "You always think you did."

The clock ticks.

A helicopter flies east over the house.

Mum is motionless in the middle of the room.

I'm jumbled and churned up inside.

"I'll get us some lunch, yeah? You've got to keep your strength up." She's already half-way out of the room.

"What do you mean, *always*?"

She says it a lot. *Always, this time, again ...*

"I've got a loaf of bread from the baker's. It'll go nicely with some chicken soup." And she flees before I can stop her.

Outside, the dull wintry sludge of the past few days has given way to bright sunshine. The leafless trees scatter into the blue sky, like spilled paint dribbling across a page. Clouds drift past the window—they have an Iridescent Gold tinge, as though they're carrying snow. But it's far too early for snow, too near the coast.

It snowed here, once. I remember making a knee-high snowman in the garden, scraping dregs of snow from the lawn and the walls. We had to climb into next door's garden when we ran out of our own.

Oh, how I've longed to be able to say *I remember* out loud, but oh how tarnished those words are. My face burns as though I'm about to cry, but there are no tears.

Mum sets a tray on the coffee table. She plumps my cushions so I'm upright and rests a bowl of soup on my lap, along with wedges of buttered bread. Not intentional wedges— she's never mastered the art of neatly slicing uncut loaves, yet she prefers the taste. I smile fondly at the recollection of barely being able to open my mouth wide enough for some of her sandwich creations. Not all memories are hard.

"How can you bear to have me here?" I ask once the meal is eaten. We've been silent the whole time; my voice cuts into the room. "I killed her. I'm a monster."

I try to connect the assorted scenes together, to create a lucid narrative. But the further I am from the dream, the fainter it is, until only the outline remains, as if penciled lines are being obliterated.

"No. Don't say that." Mum takes my bowl and stacks it into hers, fussing with the spoons and the uneaten crusts. "It's not what happened. It was ... a tragic accident."

She says nothing for a long time. She perches on the edge of the coffee table, then moves to the chair and hugs a cushion. She stares into the garden. Her mouth transforms into a frown; her eyes glaze.

"It was my fault. I got distracted. I was watching you so carefully ... I always did. But that day, I looked away. And then there were all these people ... running ..."

"But I saw it."

"It was just a dream," she says despondently. "You should rest. I think I *will* phone the doc, just in case."

I resist sleep. I resist Zenna sneaking into my head and showing me her death again. I refuse to be sucked into the nightmare. I turn on the TV and some kind of game show floods into the room. And when Mum—chewing her lip with uncertainty—comes back to say the doctor thinks there's little to be concerned about, I've settled into a post-ordeal stupor.

TWENTY-EIGHT

I paint to make sense of it all. My life empty and my life too full. I sit in front of the easel, holding a brush, and I don't know how to begin. Because it *doesn't* make sense.

I swirl my brush around the Alizarin Crimson, the bristles spreading in a fan shape. Red was a subliminal decision, but perhaps all my work from now on should be shades of blood. So I don't forget again. Because I *shouldn't* forget what I did.

I daub color across the canvas. It drips, like blood oozing from a wound.

Zenna's blood. Washing into the sea.

From my tubes of watercolors, I select Indanthrene Blue to sweep between the flecks of crimson. I take New Gamboge for the sand and cover the lower half of the canvas—it fades in and out, the uneven nature of the medium.

Occasionally, back home, Nathan would watch me work. He'd appear at the door with mugs of coffee, as though he didn't have anything better to do. When I catch movement in the corner of my eye, I illogically expect it to be him. But it's Zenna staring back—a permanent fixture in my head. No more does she vanish and reappear; no more does her voice make me start. Sometimes she's close and overbearing, forcing my brush a certain way, taking over. At others, she gazes out to sea, lost.

The red paint drools to the floor, onto the newspaper laid down to protect Mum's rug. I scoop the remainder from the palette with my fingers and smear it onto the picture. I generate ambiguous outlines, shimmering ghosts. They're slithering and vengeful, these figures—all of them Zenna, in one form or another. This is a portrait of her, for her—a true representation of what I drove her to become.

I scrape my hands down the painting, color pooling beneath my nails, snagging the canvas. All the Zennas blend together, becoming one, the way she and I are merging. I have her rage, her repugnance of me from within. The fury of being denied an existence, the chance to grow up.

***

"How did such a sweet child become so evil?" I ask.

It's much later; the room's growing dark. The half-finished painting is still on the easel—Mum and I glance at it periodically.

"She's not evil. This version of her isn't real—it's all in your head. It's your guilt twisting her this way."

"No. No," I moan, because Zenna's right here beside me, her voice a relentless presence, like waves rolling on the shore, wind rushing through trees, or a predatory hiss in tall grass. I'm fleetingly dizzy and hold my head until it passes.

"Come on, we're going out." Mum rises and expects me to do the same.

"I don't want to."

"I didn't ask. You need to get out of this house—it's not healthy to be shut away."

There's pain when I stand. I drag myself toward the hall because I don't have the impetus to argue. It's an arduous task, a long excursion, as though I'm wading through water. She won't let me forget. In the mirror, as I let Mum coerce

my arm into my coat sleeve, I'm gaunt and gray and hollow—
Zenna has superimposed herself over me, shrouding me. I
wonder if Mum sees it too.

"Not to the beach," I say as Mum locks the door.

"The pub?"

Trepidation presses into my stomach. Too far, too many
people. Too much, too soon.

"You'll be fine. We'll just have one." She touches my hand,
and I flinch. She pulls back with a troubled smile.

Mum chats lightly about her day, people she's spoken to,
how beautiful the sunrise was this morning. Her conversation muddles with Zenna's until I can't keep track of either.
My feet are soundless on the pavement, as though I'm not
walking at all.

"So …" Mum says, when we're sitting with our drinks in
front of us. She stretches her fingers out on the table, her
attention caught for a second. "Are you hungry? I am. Is it
dinner time? I never checked the time." She peers over my
shoulder. "The chocolate cake in the cabinet looks good. Is
chocolate cake dinner? I guess it can—"

"Mum, you're waffling."

She takes a breath. "Sorry."

She eyes me intently, studying me. Her fingers drum the
table. I drink, holding the glass with both hands to quell
the trembling. I smooth out the knots in my hair and shift
discomfited in my chair. Several times, she starts to say
something, then stops. She sips her own drink, while I'm
finishing off mine. I run my finger around the rim of the
glass. Just one, Mum said, but already I need another.

"Is it hard?" she asks.

"It's impossible."

"What do you want?"

"I want to close my eyes and make it stop … make *her* stop."

I close my eyes, but it doesn't stop. Zenna whispers, telling me how I held her beneath the water—how my fingers dug into her neck. She shows me the rocks; I walk toward them.

Mum downs her drink from almost two-thirds full. She shudders at the sharp sting hitting the back of her throat. She sets the glass down. "I can help with that."

Around us, the pub pauses. A glitch in time where everyone momentarily freezes—as if I could walk between the statues of fellow drinkers and reposition their hands so they'd pour beer into their laps when time begins again.

In a flash, the room is abuzz. I flinch, pulled from my daydream. Mum's still talking—her lips barely moving, concealing her words in a whisper.

"... Do you remember him?"

"Sorry, who?"

"Doctor Wheeler," she says with a hint of exasperation.

"I don't ..."

"I don't suppose it really matters."

She fumbles in her bag, pausing and staring inside, before pulling out a leaflet. It's crumpled and frayed along the folds, like it's been opened and closed many times. Her frown deepens, and she tentatively slides it toward me. She doesn't remove her hand, and I wrest it from her.

The cover shows a large house, a country hotel perhaps— MADDON HALL. It's stone-fronted with picture windows, a glass foyer, and a tree-lined gravel driveway leading up to it. Three grinning people have been amateurishly photoshopped in front of the building, pasted on with no regard for scale or harmony. Helping You Make a Fresh Start.

The gray stone portico is vaguely familiar. I have faint recollections of walking up the three wide steps to the entrance with an overriding sense of foreboding. Our thoughts are interwoven, Zenna's and mine. We both recoil.

"What's this?"

"The clinic where Doctor Wheeler works."

I flick through it, reading the trite endorsements, scanning the remarkably happy faces in the pictures. Am I supposed to be as joyful as these models?

"Have I been here?"

"Yes. He made the pain go away."

"What pain?"

Mum runs her fingernail across the grain of the table, scratching at the varnish. "The pain you're in now."

"So, it didn't work? It hasn't gone away."

She pauses, gathering her words. "For a while it did."

Craig brings two more drinks, which I'm sure we didn't order, and I'm already glugging mine as he sets Mum's in front of her. He squeezes her shoulder as he leaves. She smiles after him and returns her gaze to me, nervous and resigned.

"What do they do? How does it work?"

"They isolate the memories involved, and they remove them."

"Remove my memories? So, they took everything about my life from the age of nine?"

Mum glances away, contritely.

"No," I say, watching her avoid my eye. "Younger. I didn't know she existed." The sums are too difficult for my sleep-deprived, addled mind to handle. "Just wiped Zenna away like she never mattered? Is that what you're saying? No wonder she's pissed off." I laugh—sharp and hostile.

My stay at Maddon Hall unfolds like the petals of a flower. I'm there—we both are. Mum helps me from the car because I can't manage by myself. We stare up in amazement at this grand stately home. Vacant faces watch us from the first and second floor windows or gape blankly across the endless fields of flat countryside which surround the place.

By then, Zenna had control—paralyzing me. My only movements were ones she allowed. Bit by bit, she'd taken over and pushed me aside. My thoughts were her thoughts, and they were dark and despairing.

"Are you sure?" Mum asked. Like I had a choice.

My reflection in the windscreen no longer resembled me—my features in continual flux.

"Just get her out of my head," I whispered.

My voice was hers.

Mum heard it too.

Each step took a lifetime, each second warped as Zenna tried to impede me. Mum linked her arm with mine and bore my weight.

Inside, it was bright and airy, with Matisse prints lining the corridors. In each window and mirror we passed, I glimpsed Zenna struggling to escape. Tears rolled down our face, bereft and grieving, but my cheeks were dry. *She* was crying.

All these years I've been searching for a reason for my amnesia, and here it is. Not illness or a head trauma, or any of the other reasons Google gave me. A procedure I agreed to.

We're back in the pub with our drinks in front of us and a rendition of *Happy Birthday* floating from around the corner.

"Wait." A thought, drip-dripping into my head. So close, but elusive.

Too much commotion. I need to think. Counting the years on my fingers, fluttering them in the air as though playing a piano. So close.

"When I came home, I only remembered three or four years—nothing about university or my twenties." I run the logic out loud, but I'm talking to myself. "If Zenna was affecting me so badly, why would I wait so long?"

She runs her hands through her hair and fusses with the beer mat and squirms in her chair like a naughty child.

"Oh. Because I didn't. That wasn't the first time, was it?"

It isn't the first time Mum's explained this to me. We've been in this pub, at a different table; we've been home while I curled into the corner of my room and wept. I'm wearing different clothes; Mum's hair is long and short, brunette and auburn, and this time with a dust of gray. I lose count of the number of times we've had this conversation.

"How many?" I ask.

She takes a tortured breath. Every fact needs to be fought for, and I'm tired. "Three."

So many! I've made this decision *three times*. I've agreed people could meddle with my head, three times. And I didn't consider it to be wrong. *Three times.*

Mum watches the birthday group gathering their things and leaving. It's a sixtieth. Family members help to carry the presents and the large helium 6 and 0.

"Is it an operation?" I imagine the Swedish Chef from The Muppets arbitrarily cutting into my skull and casting aside slivers of pink brain tissue.

"No. No! I wouldn't … You take some medication and undergo a course of hypnotherapy —it's a civilized process."

I snort softly. Civilized? Not exactly the word I'd use. I stroke the edge of the leaflet until it curls. "And I'll forget you?"

She takes a moment to reply. A tear rolls down her cheek. "You'll return to your previous conviction we're estranged."

"What about my career, everything I've been working for?"

Mum shakes her head. Naturally, it will be forgotten. Or should that be, *un*naturally? I'll go back to being a barista who's fairly good at painting. Perhaps I'll move to a new place, and the manager will spot my talent and offer to hang my work on his walls. An affable lady, who may or may not have terminal cancer, will buy one or two of them and befriend me.

"What about my friends?" I hold up my hand to stop her replying because I can guess.

TWENTY-NINE

Late afternoon turns to evening. Craig collects glasses and puts out the dinner menus. He lights candles in the center of each table; Mum blows ours out and we sit in shadow.

We've stopped talking, despite there being so much more I want to say. I've been tricked, conned out of the life I should have lived. I'm half a person. The words stack up, jamming themselves into a bottleneck.

"Are you hungry?" Mum asks when I absently pick up the menu. I'm not, but I ask for chips.

While I'm sat alone, my head fills with Zenna's voice. I fight to control the agony and dread rising inside of me. I'm losing myself, becoming Zenna, having previously lost myself by ousting her. It's a stark choice—not one I want to make again.

At the bar, Mum's laughing with Craig and a couple of regulars. Not her usual laugh—she's polite and muted, glancing back to me while I stare at the beer mat and remember when I could flip five of them at once. A halo of darkness gathers around me.

"Are we drinking to oblivion then?" I ask acerbically when she returns with two more glasses.

"We've never tried it before." It's almost a joke. She smirks, but I don't.

"How does this work for you? Every time I come home you just pretend you don't know what's happening? How can you do that?"

She nods, appalled and righteous in equal measure, with a slow-burning realization in her eyes. "I don't have a choice. They can't determine how it would affect you if I blurted it all out. Doctor Wheeler says if your memories start to come back, the process should run its course. I have to wait. I have to watch you disappear piece by piece."

"Does that even make sense to you?" In the few short minutes I've been acquainted with Doctor Wheeler, I despise him. What right does he have to reprogram people, to delete their lives as though they're just a file on a computer?

"I don't pretend to understand it."

"But you're happy to put me through it again?"

"I don't put you through anything." Her voice rises. Several people glance up from their meals and conversations. Mum shrinks into her seat. "*You* chose this. *You* found the website, and you showed me, and *you* begged *me*."

It's too big; I can't handle this. Zenna laughs—in my head and all around. Mum balls her hands into a fist, and I wonder if she hears her too.

"But I forget *everything*. I forget you—I leave you alone."

"I have friends," she says lightly. "Craig," she adds in a deeper, warmer tone. "And you have Nathan. Mothers and daughters who don't speak aren't uncommon—we're no different to lots of other families."

"Stop it!" The couple on the next table stare; I smile apologetically. "Wait. Nathan knows about this? You *know* Nathe?" I'm winded, punched in the stomach. How much more of this shit can there be!

"I do. He contacted me a long time ago. You were at uni, suffering, and he didn't know what to do. It was the first time, so it was new to us all—I was so scared for you."

Mum leans back in her chair so the barmaid can put our plates down. She thanks her and asks after her parents, then turns back to me. "He keeps me in the loop. He helps you more than you realize. He's a good man."

He is. But he knows. He can't—he'd have said something. He wouldn't just let me suffer. Yet, he has—that's exactly what he's done. I've poured my heart out to him, and he's heard it all before but said nothing. And then reported back to my mother!

The leaflet is more crumpled than it was—did I screw it up in fury? The people on the front are laughing, mocking me with their empty heads and unencumbered lives. And I'm there again, inhaling the scent of antiseptic and fear, hearing people wailing in their rooms. Covering my head with my pillow to muffle the tears and screams as their demons are yanked out of them. I observe the compliant zombies they become, and I'm one of them.

"This is so fucked up. Our lives all shaken up over something which doesn't even work. Can't you see it? Are you in so deep you don't even question it anymore?"

"I hate what Zenna does to you, what she's *doing* to you. She's not your sister. You create her. Your guilt manifests into something hideous. When Selena died—you wouldn't talk, you buried your grief so deep, it became too much for you to handle. You were nine, of course it was too much. I should have done so much more for you."

She takes a chip and swirls it into the ketchup. She drifts away, jolting herself back with a sorrowful smile.

"You were right though—she *was* your imaginary friend for a long time, and she was real for you. You were about fifteen, sixteen when you discovered the clinic and asked me to help you. You said she was still talking to you, and I knew we had to try something drastic."

She's not imaginary, she's not my guilt manifested. She's

inside me, forcing herself into every crevice of my body. She's pushing me out, overpowering me. I'm disappearing; I'm an empty vessel, a pencil sketch being slowly erased. She's haunting me from within.

My head fills with Zenna's voice, a loud crescendo of laughter and contempt. I stumble from the pub and out into the cold, dismal night.

The clouds break in small patches and stars flicker. I lean on the sea wall and stare into the blackness. Lights from ships on the horizon flicker. They change color while I stare at them, although it's just an illusion, just my eyes playing tricks.

I want to stand on the sand, one last time—feel the pebbles grind underfoot and dance with the waves. Would it be the last, or will I be back here next year, the one after that, asking the same questions, suffering the same anguish? Can denying Zenna existed be right? After all these years, doesn't she deserve better? Mum says we've got no choice. And Zenna, inside my head, begs me not to suppress her again.

I want to stand on the sand, but it scares me. Like on my first day, when the world spun around me.

Mum followed me from the pub. She's behind me, probably with my bag and coat which I left in my haste to be liberated. It's cold; my breath curls on the frosty air, but I don't turn. I don't take my coat from her.

She rests against the wall, looking toward the road rather than the water. She takes a packet of cigarettes from her bag and slides one out. She turns it between her fingers for a moment before lighting it. "We should have moved away. Maybe none of this would have happened. We could have had a fresh start. But my baby died here, I couldn't leave her."

Heartache and anxiety circle the hills; death lurks in the water.

"Every time you come home," she continues, "I think I'll be able to handle it, that it'll be different this time." She smiles ruefully and blows smoke into the wind. "I live with it every single day, but I forget each time is the first for you."

Every time, each of the three times, she loses a second daughter while reliving the death of the first. No one takes her memories away. She deals with it all alone. Why do I get special treatment?

"Why did you let me do it?"

"The first time? I genuinely thought it would help you move on. It seemed no more drastic than the counseling you'd had before. When I spoke to Doctor Wheeler, he pushed the counseling side of it." She pauses and frowns, watching her own private film playing in front of her. "I didn't fully under-stand the implications—I just wanted to make you better."

She flicks ash, takes one last drag, and stamps the ciga-rette into the pavement.

"Your delusions have been getting stronger over time. This is the worst I've seen you, though—you've never ended up in hospital, this is new." There's so much she's trying to say, bunching it up inside her. The torment is gouged into her face.

"What if she's real? You say *delusion* like it's all in my head. But?"

She shakes her head adamantly. "Ghosts aren't real." She stares up at the stars. "Not my Selena."

I follow her gaze. "How does it work?"

I've asked before; I've gone through it. But the details never stick. Zenna wheedles into my head, burrowing into me, discarding the memories she doesn't want me to retain.

"We call the clinic ... whenever you're ready."

We stand side-by-side, listening to the waves. When I look closely, Zenna's turning cartwheels on the sand.

THIRTY

When I wake, I'm in yesterday's clothes—a faint odor of sea-salt hangs from them. I long for my own bed, for its comfort and the way it sags in just the right spot, for Nathan in the kitchen calling through to tell me the coffee's ready. I wish I'd never come here. Although, having the truth—again—is a relief. A *relief*, really? Perhaps not. Is there any difference between losing my mind and having it stolen from me?

Four canvases are stacked against the chest of drawers, the canvases I've used this past week. They'll be waiting for my return, too. Mum will take them from the cupboard under the stairs and offer them to me as though they're her own. And I'll paint over them, again.

My bags are half-packed; my clothes shoved into them last night in a rage, before I fell, exhausted, onto the bed. Mum hasn't phoned the clinic yet, but I think I'm ready.

Zenna's beside me and in front of me and all around me and inside me. Our hearts beat in unison; my hand is her hand as we fumble for my mobile to video call Nathan.

"Jo? How's it going?"

His face on screen freezes briefly before lurching and pixelating as he moves.

My words fail. I have so much to say, I'm not sure I'll fit them all in. Once I start, they'll be a deluge of indiscernible noise.

"You knew," I say at last. "All this time, you knew."

His bright smile turns into a frown, with a deep crevice between his brows. His shoulders sag, with comprehension. "Yes."

How long has he been expecting this call? Has he stayed home day after day, just in case? Or been out enjoying himself with his girlfriend, the one whose name I can never remember? A stupid question—he's allowed to go out and do whatever he likes. We don't owe each other anything.

And yet, I find myself saying, "You lied to me."

"No, I never lied."

"*Three times*, Nathan!" Exasperation rather than rage. What's the point of anger? I've been angry before—it's never made any difference. We still end up back here.

I was incensed the first time, at Nathan, at my mother. I hated they'd united to create this bizarre illusion of my life. Lying to me, hiding my own past from me. They had no idea how it felt to discover everyone around me knew more about me than I did. My perception of myself was ripped away. Everything I believed was fake. Now, it's simply surreal; I shrug off the inevitability.

"Twice, for me," he says. "I met you after you had your first treatment. You were sitting beneath a tree, sketching people. You were ... enigmatic."

He stood over me, and I was irritated because he created a shadow across my page. When I looked up to confront him, his face was a silhouette—it took a second for my eyes to adjust. He was cute, but cocky, wearing a Guns N' Roses t-shirt and torn jeans.

"You were different from anyone else I'd ever met," he continues, while I'm lost in my reverie. "Aloof and cool—in a compelling way, of course. I asked you out for a drink."

I said he wasn't my type. But we were on the same art course and we became friends despite my first impression.

"Because of it, surely," he says, with a goofy grin.

I shrug off the nostalgia. "You can skip to the part where you colluded with my mother."

"That's not fair—you've heard it before. You know this."

"I want you to tell me again." I need to know if the stories have changed over time.

He blows out a long breath, whistling without the sound. "You were having nightmares, horrible ones. You woke up screaming in the night, inconsolable. Your painting style became dark and hostile. You were painting Zenna over and over—you said you had to get her out of your head. You stopped eating, struggled with your coursework. But you wouldn't talk about it.

"I called your mother. I found her number, through a bit of trial and error, and ..." he stops, glancing to his left, out of his window I imagine. Perhaps someone's talking loudly, or a car alarm is bleating out.

"And she told you a lot more than you bargained for," I say, to remind him he's only part way through. It's no longer shocking he snooped around behind my back.

"Sorry, yes, she did. I'd wondered if you had some health stuff going on, not taking your medication or ... It wouldn't have mattered, but wow—I wasn't expecting ..."

"Why didn't you tell me?"

"When?"

"The first time."

"Your mum begged me not to, said the treatment was supposed to be permanent. It had only been four years by then, but it was starting to wear off. She was worried too much info would set off some kind of mental spiral. That's what the clinic told her."

"Did you believe her?"

He pinches the bridge of his nose. "I had no reason not to. The nightmares got worse. You went home, *looking for answers*." He makes quote marks with his fingers.

"I always come back here, don't I?"

"You decided to undergo the treatment again. We'd been together three years. I visited you before you went to the clinic—you were so pale and thin, I barely recognized you. Your mum explained what would happen, and that you probably wouldn't know me afterwards."

I remember loving him. I remember having no memory of him. Both realities are nestled side-by-side.

"Are you coming down this time?"

"Do you want me to?"

"There's no point, is there? You'll let me do it anyway."

"That's not fair." His voice cracks, and he coughs to recover himself. "When you came back to London, you were you again, the woman I saw beneath the tree. The one before she fell in love with me. Some of your hypnotherapy sessions had placed the notion we were flatmates, and I felt I had to go along with it. What would you have done? I wanted you to be safe, to look after you. You were so disorientated and vulnerable, naturally—you'd never have survived by yourself."

I recall the ring, tucked away in the box beneath my bed. "We were engaged. *You* gave me the ring."

He's down on one knee. We're in the walled garden at Lyme Park, away for the weekend. It's raining, but it doesn't deter him. He's been planning this for weeks, he'll tell me later—he's not going to let the weather interfere.

He's somber and forlorn, lost in the memory.

I'd said yes when he proposed, and it knotted me into his sense of obligation.

It's selfish; I'm selfish for even considering it. Around me, people suffer a lot more than I do—awaiting the return of someone who doesn't exist anymore. Nathan should have moved on years ago. He shouldn't be babysitting an ex-girlfriend who doesn't even know she's an *ex*. If he were anyone else, he'd be long gone.

And Mum ... my poor grief-stricken mother, stuck here, because she can never predict when I might turn up on her doorstep and start this whole thing off again.

Zenna sits beside me and laughs, with cruelty and mockery. I catch our reflection in the mirror—my face veiled by hers, our features mutating.

"Jo? I love you. I always will."

"But you *shouldn't*. How can you live like this?" Inside, I'm screaming, but I don't have the energy. Why can't they see it? What's wrong with them? "I'm going to forget you again. You can't go on like this."

I've said it all before. The previous versions of me are converging—perched on the chair in the corner of the room, or half-way up the stairs. We're telling Nathan we can't love him.

"Someone needs to look after you when you leave the clinic, someone who understands."

"You're a freak," I say harshly and cover my mouth, shocked something so horrible could tumble out.

He presses his palms together, in primary school prayer, and chews his index fingers. "Is that what you think?"

"I don't know ... No, of course it isn't."

Zenna squeals and claps her hands together. *Yes, oh yes, a freak, a weirdo. Go on, tell him again, tell him he makes your skin crawl ...*

"I'm scared, Nathe. What should I do?"

He takes his time. "Zenna consumes you. She absorbs you until you're just a shadow and have no choice."

"So, I can't fight her?"

Can't fight, can't run from the ghost burrowing into me. Can't do anything.

"Talk to me."

"We are talking."

"Not about this. Just talk."

I curl myself around my pillow as he chats self-consciously about his work, and the band he saw last night with friends. He says my paintings have almost all sold. The gallery is interested in more. And then he pauses because there won't be more.

And I remember how much I love him, and how I'll never have the life with him we both deserve. Because once I reach this stage, there's nothing left of me. I'm Zenna, and I will be again.

THIRTY-ONE

I'm on the pitch-black beach and have no idea how I got here.

The blue-tinged moon catches on the tips of waves, and the houses clinging to the hill around me are Christmas-lit. In London, the Oxford Street lights would have been switched on weeks ago. Nathan and I would have wandered around the shops, wrapped up against the cold winds, stopping for hot chocolate and roasted chestnuts.

I didn't say goodbye when I was on the phone to him. This version of myself should have said goodbye, before the new one says hello. All the discussion, all the debate and tears and guilt, meant nothing—it was inevitable, as if I were at the summit of an icy slope and letting myself slowly slide to the bottom.

It's stormy; the edge of a hurricane is stirring up the surf. I keep to the edges, close to the cliff where the lights from the high road shine onto the sand. As I walk further into darkness, I use the torch on my phone, stumbling as the sand turns to pebbles. Spray hits my face, and I jolt.

"We loved to play here, didn't we?" Zenna asks, solid and unflinching beside me. "Long after the last tourists had packed up and gone home. Hats and coats and boots, splashing in the rockpools." She nudges my arm, amiably. "I know you remember."

"Please leave me alone." My words are futile. There's no longer any distinction between us—our symbiosis is complete.

"Why can't we share our childhood? We're the only two people who truly appreciate how much fun we had."

I slump through the shingle to sit on a heavy square rock at the base of the cliff. I'd run, if I could, but she'd find me.

"After all," she continues, light and singsong, "if I was alive, we'd be meeting for coffee, and shopping, and going away for weekend breaks together. Wouldn't we?"

Nathan goes fishing with his brother. Lily meets hers for dinner once a month or so.

"I guess."

"It's what I want for us—you and me together, always."

"This isn't fair. You shouldn't be doing this to me. It's time for you to rest."

"I understand," she says forlornly, resentfully. "I don't matter. My life means nothing to you."

"No, that's not ..."

But she's gone.

"... what I meant," I yell into the wind, and my words are hurled around by the ferocious gusts.

I'm wrenched from her, a searing pain. Ahead, there's nothing but darkness and a gaping hole where my sister should be. A girl with whom I should have grown into womanhood—an ally, a best friend, an occasional adversary. Someone who I'd always be able to depend on.

Just an accident, Mum continues to say. And sometimes, I believe her.

And sometimes I speculate if—on that terrifying day— Zenna had annoyed me so much I wanted to shut her up, just for a moment. My touch really was a shove, delivered in rage. My rush to help her masked by my unconscious desire to push her under.

I was the elder sibling. I was supposed to take care of her. *It was just an accident.*

Horrid thoughts run around my head, circling themselves, forming realities and narratives out of half-remembered scraps. They mingle with Zenna's, altering history based on my guilt and regret.

"Watch me!"

Oh, her voice, her eagerness. She was always up to something. I remember Mum rolling her eyes and her *what now* expression. What now, is Zenna's high up the cliff, almost at the fence of the garden which backs onto the edge. What now, is she's gripping with all her might as soil and stones crumble and sprinkle over me.

"Zenna, come down. Mum says we've got to be home before the tide turns."

"Don't wanna. Ooh, they've got chickens." She clucks like a chicken. "Come and look, Jo-Jo."

This never happened. This is brand new tonight.

I scramble up after her. Wind blusters around me, buffeting me against the sharp shale.

It was dark when I was on the beach, but now it's midday, midsummer. I'm nine and my sister is six, and she isn't dead yet.

She monkey-climbs sideways and hangs from the wooden fence which is rickety and at an angle due to erosion. I cling to the edge, to the loose rock crumbling beneath my fingers.

"Take my hand," Zenna says, stretching down to me. "I want to show you something."

I don't trust her. But she's no longer the maleficent adult of my nightmares. She's every sweet, blonde-haired photo Mum has of her. Her cheeks are full and reddened with the effort of her ascent. I hesitate and peer down at the ragged rocks and sheer drop.

"You'll fall. Take my hand, Jo-Jo, please."

And I do. She lifts me far easier than she ought to, and I thump onto the grassy tuft beside her—my heart palpitating, my breathing erratic.

Beyond the headland, a flash of lightning illuminates the distant clouds and a low grumble ricochets off the hills. Above us, the sun is still bright and hot. Our faces glow with joy, and Zenna's contented as she gazes out over the ocean.

"I've never been this high before," she says.

I have. Afterwards. After she died. While everyone stood unblinking in somber funeral clothes, I slipped from the house and climbed. I ignored the ache in my stomach and tears I couldn't control, concentrating on my hands and feet moving in unison, one after the other after the other. So focused I didn't notice how high I was getting. The cliff hadn't eroded so much, back then, there was a choice of gardens to aim for. At the top, I flopped onto my back and reached out to the clouds zipping past, as though they might dip down and scoop me up. Zenna was above them, in Heaven, and I wanted to be with her.

She points out the boat crossing the bay, lurching on the waves, its white sail billowing.

"I'm going to sail around the world when I grow up," she says. And after a moment, "I'm going to be a famous swimmer."

She could be, could have been. A little fish, more confident in the water than me.

"Look at the waves." She stares straight down. "Look at the water. Isn't it beautiful? We should dive."

There's no water. The sea doesn't come this far up the beach. It's just sand and pebbles, assuming we dived with an arc rather than dropping feet first onto the rocks.

"See how blue it is, like ... the necklace Mummy wears."

Sapphire. Mum wears a sapphire pendant on a silver chain. She bought it in memory of Zenna on what would have been her eighteenth birthday.

"There's no water—"

"Look, really *look*," she demands. "It's so clear, I can see right to the bottom. It's so deep, we wouldn't even touch the bottom." She leans forward with her arms held out to balance herself.

There's no water this far up the beach, but I see it. Bright and clear on this midsummer day. Splashing and swirling around the rockpools, serenading us.

Zenna holds my hand and helps me to my feet. "Are you scared?"

Side-by-side, my sister and me, the way it should have been. Her hand is so soft and small in mine. She looks up at me with bright amber eyes. It's not right; it's not her. It's never been her.

I step forward, my foot slipping a little. I stare down. There's no water. "Yes," I say with a smirk. "Aren't you?"

"I don't get scared." The adult Zenna's voice in the child's body.

"You should be. Without me, there'll be no you." I squeeze her hand tightly and resist her pulling away from me—the adult Zenna trying to take control again. Not this time, not again.

I inch forward, lining myself up. I take a breath, a last appraisal of the horizon. Without me, there'll be no Zenna. More than anything, I want her to leave me alone. This is better than losing myself again, better than finding out all over again.

"Jo-Jo ..." Her voice quivers.

For once, I'm in control.

And I jump. I dive. I drag Zenna with me.

For one brief moment, we're perfectly synchronized. Our bodies arc and our limbs twist and reach into the air.

We don't land. We fly forever.

THIRTY-TWO

I sketch our lives together, the images appearing in graphite lines and pastel shades. Page after page.

Two little girls play on the beach at the tail end of summer. Two sisters jumping in and out of the soft waves crawling back and forth over the sand. Zenna and I, giggling as a surge catches us unaware and sweeps our legs from beneath us.

Zenna swims to the rocks, our little fish. She's at the very top of them and eyes me defiantly—she knows she's being naughty. She's testing me because Mum's dozing on the sand under her big straw hat.

I scramble across. *No,* I tell her. *We're not allowed to jump, it's naughty and you'll hurt yourself.*

My mother's words parroted from my mouth.

Zenna hesitates, her arms poised overhead in perfect diving position, and I don't know what to do.

Look at the rocks sticking out of the water, I say. *If you hurt yourself, you won't be able to go to ballet on Friday.* I'm running out of reasons, but she hasn't jumped—she's waiting for a better one. *Mummy said we can choose a cake on the way home, remember?*

She grins and climbs back down, jumping into my arms. For a six-year-old, she's tiny, and I easily carry her all the way back to Mummy. I glance back at the rocks as Mum packs our picnic basket. I half-expect them to look different somehow, more ragged and sinister.

***

The summer ends, and school starts again. New uniform—too big, with the starchiness of being unworn. For Christmas, I get a proper grown-up easel and paints you squeeze from the tubes. Zenna joins a swimming club. The year passes, another summer comes and goes. I move up to the big school. After several attempts, Zenna wins her first race and wants to be called Selena from now on. Her name starts to appear in local papers and her coach suggests she's good enough to try out for the county team.

I pass my exams with acceptable grades—not as high as Mum and Dad hoped, not as low as I feared. I get a place at art college. Selena passes hers with much better grades than me, and I go to university in London.

Selena swims at national level while trying to keep her A-Levels going. In the end she has to choose, and she chooses swimming.

I meet Nathan. I'm sitting beneath a tree on campus, eating lunch and sketching people. I've not made many friends, so I spend a lot of my time in this manner. He stands over me, casting a shadow, and says hello.

On Selena's eighteenth birthday, Mum gives her a sapphire pendant on a silver chain. It's her birthstone. I'm a little envious because my birthstone is a pearl, and it reminds me of old ladies in tweed jackets, so my pendant is in my jewelry box and I only wear it at Christmas. This gift, around Selena's neck, makes her eyes shine—it's perfect for her.

She joins the England swim team for the world championships. Nathan and I watch her compete in the rounds, and then the finals. I hold my breath as she inches closer and closer to the German woman in the lead. We're in the stands with Mum and Dad and hug each other when she wins bronze in the 800m Freestyle.

Months pass. Memories are made. I conduct my first post-university solo art exhibition to rave reviews. They're abstract pieces, inspired by the Cornish coast. Next, I planned to work on some self-portraits, but they're not going well—they don't look like me. So I ditch them for something else.

When we meet up, especially in London, we cause a stir— the famous swimmer and her emerging artist sister. We're pictured in the tabloids leaving restaurants or waiting for trains, as though it's somehow interesting or newsworthy.

One day, she phones to tell me she's met someone, and she's pregnant. We go together to tell our parents—even though she's twenty-four, she's worried they'll be angry. But they're delighted. I wait a few months before I announce my engagement so I don't overshadow her.

I meet my nephew for the first time at my wedding. Selena is new-mum exhausted but smiles in the photos and dotes on her son. She's already in training again, but it's harder than she thought.

We gather at Christmases and birthdays, weddings and Christenings—all the big ones.

My art career develops with further exhibitions and worldwide sales. I have a child of my own and paint while he sleeps. After a raft of gold medals, Selena retires from swimming through injury and returns to Cornwall. She shrugs off our concern and claims it was the right time. When her son is five, she announces she's single again and starts coaching the county swim team. Occasionally she's asked to pundit on the BBC, and ends up doing Strictly Come Dancing, crashing out during movie week.

I have another boy, and everyone asks when I'll be trying for a girl.

Sometimes I catch myself staring at Selena—in awe of her confidence and poise. I sketch her newly cropped hair and her fledgling wrinkles. *You could make me a little younger*, she remonstrates. But I think she's beautiful just the way she is. She swims laps before the team starts training and meets a widower with an eight-year-old daughter.

Years pass: memories are made. Nathan and I move back to Cornwall when we feel too old for the tumult of London. I'm comfortably famous.

I'm forty, then fifty. The colors change—vibrant shades of red and orange become soft and calm. Our lives settle into an easy rhythm. My studio is a large room with doors opening onto a balcony. At the end of the day, Nathan brings glasses of wine and we sit out there, hand-in-hand.

The boys grow up and leave home. Selena and I walk the coast path together and eat far too much cake at National Trust houses. Nathan and I travel.

Dad dies at a good age. Selena and I take turns caring for Mum—going on daytrips and having her over for dinner. She's lost without him, and a year later, she sits down to watch TV and doesn't get up again.

We're in the rain beside her grave—our kids bear our weight, and we're grateful we have each other. And afterwards, we sit together and remember.

***

I draw these things, this life which never was, to make sense of it all. Page after page, from my hospital bed; my tribute to the girl who never grew up.

When I was stretchered from the beach that harrowing day, weeks ago, they left Zenna behind. Both of us fell on the network of boulders designed to shore up the cliff face, our broken bodies tangled among the rocks, but only I was pulled out and swept away by the air ambulance—my leg shattered, my jaw and collarbone broken. I tried to tell them she was there, but she wasn't anymore. She wasn't inside me; she wasn't anywhere.

Lucky to be alive, they said. My leg is held together in a metal cage. My food is cut into tiny pieces before it comes to me; I need help guiding the fork to my mouth. Lucky, they said.

It's quiet without Zenna's unremitting presence. Inside not out. Outside is full of all the usual commotion. Footsteps and conversations and trolleys and wheels and engines and purring and sirens and beeps and coughs. Each sound is an aria unfolding into a vibrant opera.

She's Selena now. My childhood name for her is sullied. *Zenna* is a relic, a fantasy torn from our symbiotic torture and buried at the bottom of the cliff. Selena is forever young and beloved, the victim of a tragic accident, to be remembered and mourned.

I open the pad to the final page, blank and expansive, but I still don't know what the final scene should be.

THIRTY-THREE

I'm allowed home on the day it snows. It starts with a
flutter, caught on tree branches and the roofs of cars,
dancing from the sky.

Nathan says we should get a move on. He glances outside,
frowning as the world turns gray and the snowfall intensifies. "It's getting heavier."

"It won't be snowing at Mum's."

"It's snowed on your beach before. I saw the pictures."

"Years ago." I wasn't there. I was in a bubble of amnesia,
months away from drawing Zenna for the "first" time. But
I saw the footage spread across the news. In another life,
Selena, Mum, and I might have rushed down to the beach
and thrown snowballs with our neighbors.

"Yeah," Nathan says, his attention divided between the
clock on the wall and the flurry outside.

The drive home is slow and steady. Nathan checks if
I'm okay, if I'm comfortable, if I want the heating turned
higher—an onslaught of politeness and awkwardness.

We haven't talked properly yet. A hospital ward isn't the
best place for a heart-to-heart, with the sound of Radio 4
interviews floating between our curtained-off cubicles and
the distraction of nurses attending to my fellow patients.
This is the first time we've been alone.

He hurtled down from London when he heard about my *accident*. Not accident, I want to say. My fall, perhaps, my jump, my finale.

He sat beside my bed while I drifted in and out of consciousness, imagining he was another delusion. He curled into the fetal position on pushed-together chairs in the waiting room until Mum persuaded him to go home with her. He was holding my hand when I regained full cognizance, when I realized he was exactly the person I wanted to see.

Does it mean he still loves me? Does it mean I love him, or should love him, or owe it to him to love him? Do we pick up the wedding preparations from where we left them or shake hands and say goodbye?

So many questions. No answers.

The clouds darken; snow falls faster. It collects in mounds at the side of the road and obscures the pavements but lightens as we get closer to the coast—melting as it hits the road and turning to sludge on the windscreen. We sweep around the final corner onto the sea front, and my gaze is drawn to the water, to the frothing, foaming waves and the cloud-covered horizon.

Nathan helps me out of the car and carries me up the steps from the road to Mum's front lawn. So easy to skip up as a seven-year-old, challenging after my long overnight drive from London, impossible with an unwieldy cast and wayward crutches. He lifts me easily and hugs me tight against his chest.

***

I wish everything was as neatly tied up as the life I drew for Selena. I turn the pages of the sketchpad and stare at her lined, matured face, and the streaks of gray I gave her for her fortieth birthday.

With the injuries I sustained, I no longer resemble my own depiction. The book is a fiction for both of us. My left cheek is still slightly swollen, tight when I chew or speak; the bruises are Yellow Oxide, fading from their previous Vivid Lime Green. Deep, snaking scars where I hit the rocks are Naphthol Crimson, but they'll lighten to silver eventually.

In front of the mirror, I touch the glass rather than my own skin. Cold, smooth, perfectly formed glass.

***

"I'd like to visit the cemetery," I say at dinner. So far, we've adeptly avoided the subject. The longer Selena's name is unspoken, the further away we push her.

Mum and Nathan glance at each other, knives and forks set down. I cut my chicken into tiny pieces and pretend I can't sense their hesitation.

"Are you sure?"

To lay flowers on the grave of my baby sister, of course I am. To visit the scene of such previous horror and torment, tangled with a malignant force, knowing I was on the way back to the place where my whole life would be wiped away again, I'm less certain.

But I flash a smile and take a breath and say, "Yes. I want to."

The following day, we wrap up against the icy westerly wind. Nathan stays behind to cook dinner for our return. It's Craig's night off, so he'll join us. He might arrive early, bringing leftover cheesecake from the pub, and they'll have a beer together.

It's crisp when we get out of the car at the cemetery. Remnants of snow still gather in the roots of trees and around gravestones; it sparkles like magic in the sunlight. The serenity of the churchyard sweeps over us. The silence is punctuated with the rustle of branches and the faint chirping of birds. For the first time in months, I'm at peace.

I hobble along, still not used to the concentration needed for crutches. They catch on weeds growing at the side of the path or where the root of a tree is lifting tarmac. The sun shines in defined lines through the clouds, hitting some of the newer white marble headstones so they glow like angels.

Selena's red granite stone, when we reach it, is tarnished and dull; the engraved script is obscured by small clumps of wilting brown moss.

"Oh, my poor baby," Mum says, crouching scratching the moss away and tracing the lettering with her finger. "I meant to come back sooner, but ..."

But her days and months passed as she picked up the pieces I'd left behind once more. And it was never the right moment, and her strength ebbed away. We all hid in our own way, from the past and the inevitable future.

"We'll come again together. We'll bring a trowel and dig up the weeds properly."

She nods, pulling randomly at some of the creeping dandelion stalks and sweeping the mulch of dead leaves from the base, with the same idleness she used to tidy my bedroom while she was talking to me. *Sorry*, she'd say when I whined at her to leave my things alone. *It's a mum thing.*

Mud stains her fingers, and she wipes them on her jeans. She peels the plastic wrapper from the pink carnations we bought, shoving it into her pocket, and hands them to me. I bend as best I can to lay them one-by-one in front of the stone.

"There, that's better, isn't it? Pink ones, your favorite. Sorry I haven't been for a while. I promise to come more often." She wipes a tear, but her voice is warm and happy. "Jo-Jo's here. Um, it snowed a couple of days ago. I expect this place was covered. You'd have loved it, Selena, it was so pretty."

I take a step away and watch her in admiration. After so long only thinking about myself, this is the way it should always have been—the two of us sharing our pain. There's a contentment in her I haven't seen for a long time. Eventually she stands.

"Do you want ... shall I leave you alone for a while? I can sit in the car and wait for you."

"Can you hold my hand?"

We stand in contemplation and reflection. There's something about the vacuum of the churchyard which gives solace and equanimity. I absorb it, allowing it to flow through me. Memories rise and linger. Good ones, now, only the best. I smile and feel the warmth of small arms around my waist.

My leg starts to ache, and my arms are stiff with the pressure of the crutches.

"Nathan needs to go home soon," I say, watching the sun move lower in the sky. I've lost track of time, but the days are still short, and the darkness is always abrupt. "I've decided to go with him."

She nods. "As you should."

"You're not upset?"

"I'll miss you." She tucks a stray hair into my woolly hat. "But you'll phone me and visit whenever you want. I'll come to London. I knew you wouldn't be staying for good." She tries to smile, to be jolly and upbeat. "You have a life to get back to, a studio you must be longing to work in again."

"I work in my bedroom, it's hardly something to crave."

"Maybe not for long, eh?" She raises her eyebrows and smiles mischievously.

"You mean ...?" I blush. "We haven't talked about it. He hasn't said anything. He may not even ..."

"Take your time. You've got a lot to work through."

"Do you think we can? It feels like it'll all go wrong as soon as we start analyzing it. I'm not sure I can trust him anymore."

"Oh Jo ..." She lifts her head and stares at the passing clouds. They move briskly in a wind more tumultuous up there than down on the ground. "Nathan loves you. If you love him, you'll work it out."

"I called him a freak."

She stifles a giggle. "I've called Craig names. I called your father much worse, even when we were happy." She checks her watch. "Are you ready? It'll be dark soon, and you must be freezing."

As we make our way along the path, I turn back to Selena's headstone. The last time I left her behind, a dark shadow fell across the grave—Zenna watching intently, waiting for the cycle to begin again. Now birds sing from the thick branches of the sycamore tree, and soft pink clouds hint at the beautiful pastel sunset to come.

I hold on to this moment; I note every detail. Later, when I draw it, perhaps it'll be the final page.

ACKNOWLEDGEMENTS

I am so excited to see Jo out in the world. She's been through a lot in the twenty years since she arrived, fully formed, in my head, tugging at my sleeve until I told her story. Along the way, I've had the help of my three amazing critique partners—Elizabeth Seckman, Ruth Schiffmann, and Nick Wilford. I'm not sure what I'd do without their unique insights, each of them offering something slightly different to the process, and all of them essential.

Thanks to Jessica Bell and Amie McCracken, the most supportive and passionate publishers an author could wish for; to Melanie Faith, my editor for this book, for her unwavering excitement for the story, and all her little comments in the margins; and to Peter Snell, the VLP acquisitions guru who saw the potential.

For readers who know Cornwall well, you might recognize Seaton as being the inspiration for the village and beach which is unnamed in the novel. Over years of walking my dog there and stopping for hot chocolate and buttered teacakes afterwards, the setting took shape. "Research" is a great excuse for doing many things, especially drinking hot chocolate on a sunny winter's day!

As always, the biggest shout out goes to my family and my friends, who are always there for me and are well aware that at certain points of a novel I'm going to lose track of a conversation because my characters are talking to me as well.

This book, and all future books, will be in loving memory of my dad, who—despite not being a big reader of fiction—encouraged me every step of the way.

VINE LEAVES PRESS

Enjoyed this book?
Go to *vineleavespress.com* to find more.

9 781925 965650